I0722185

KISS AND KILL IN TEXAS

An Al Quinn Novel

RUSS HALL

Kiss and Kill in Texas
Red Adept Publishing, LLC
104 Bugenfield Court
Garner, NC 27529
https://RedAdeptPublishing.com/
Copyright © 2022 by Russ Hall. All rights reserved.
Cover Art by Streetlight Graphics[1]
No part of this book may be reproduced, scanned, or distributed in any printed or electronic form without permission. Please do not participate in or encourage piracy of copyrighted materials in violation of the author's rights. Thank you for respecting the hard work of this author.

This is a work of fiction. Names, characters, places, and incidents either are the product of the author's imagination or are used fictitiously, and any resemblance to locales, events, business establishments, or actual persons—living or dead—is entirely coincidental.

A good story is comprised of contrast—extreme contrast—and there is no greater yin versus yang than life or death. –Al Quinn

Chapter One

Al Quinn had the motor on his bass boat cranked up as fast as it could go. The breeze across Lake Travis was already putting a chop on the greenish-blue water, making rows of whitecaps. The wakes of half a dozen Jet Skis, boats towing water-skiers, and some boats just going "flat out stupid" sent cross waves that turned the water's surface into dips, hollows, and sharp peaks that snow skiers would call moguls.

Fergie reached over from where she sat beside him and put a hand on his shoulder. She couldn't say anything. Any words would be lost in the wind. Her long red hair fanned out behind her. The wind had snapped Al's ball cap off a while back, but he hadn't slowed to go back for it.

The first thing he'd said after hanging up his cell phone was "I wonder what that damned fool wants and why he thinks it's so damned urgent." But he'd fired up his boat and pulled out of a cove where they'd been having pretty good luck catching bass.

He could see the boat ramp at Muleshoe Bend just ahead but couldn't make out a figure standing near it yet.

His blood surged through him in a flame-hot adrenaline rush. He took shallow breaths while bending forward to see through the spray of mist that rushed at him over the bow as the boat bounced up and down. They caught air a couple of times, only to slap down in hard thumps that nearly shot Fergie out of her seat.

He'd pushed the speed of his boat more than he liked, all the way across the lake from where they'd been fishing. Fergie had nearly been tossed several times, once when she reached forward to tighten the bungee cords holding the fishing rods in place on the deck. Since then, she'd kept a one-handed death grip on the rail of the console.

As they neared the boat ramp, he could see the outer end of it didn't quite reach the water. The lake's water level was low and had been dropping, which meant less space for the boats using it. The upper end of the ramp was closed and marked off by orange cones. The waves of their wake began to echo off the shore and bounce back to move their bow up and down even as Al slowed to get a better look.

A row of a dozen black buzzards stretched their wings out toward the sun on the brown grass of one slope. *No reason to read anything like an omen into that.*

As he was peering from one side of the park to the other, Fergie shouted, "There he is!"

At last, Al spotted Bobby Ray Champion, who stood as still as a statue, waiting for them, one jeans-clad leg leaning against a cement picnic table.

"We're in time," Al said.

As soon as he said it, Bobby Ray's neck gave a jerk, his whole body twitched, and a spray of blood spatter erupted where one eye had been. His body relaxed as it toppled forward onto the grass. The buzzards took off in a frantic flutter of black wings.

"Get ready to take the wheel!" Al yelled.

He backed off the power and let the boat slide beside the pilings until his starboard bow bumped against the wood. Al jumped onto his seat and leaped onto the dock. His feet went at a full run as soon as they hit the boards. He nearly stumbled crossing a grit-sprinkled plank to the shore, but he caught himself and ran faster as he crossed some gravel and started across the grass.

Al did not stop at Bobby Ray or even look down at him as he ran past. He was calculating and searching the distance. Depending on who held the rifle and what kind of experience they had at long range, the shooter was probably three hundred to five hundred feet away. Although if the shooter was a pro, Al could guess the distance as far as a thousand feet, even with a breeze. He glanced at the nearest trees and saw their tops swaying. A stiff wind like that might shorten the shooting distance for some. It would have to be factored into the shot.

He kept running as fast as he could go, taking in the possibilities. He was looking for slightly higher ground and a lane of fire where a bullet could travel without clipping a tree limb. A line of raised rocks that looked like a low balcony to his right seemed the best position.

A stitch in his left side stabbed at him, but he sought to ignore it as he ran on, though he did slow a bit, holding his side. He jogged and took walks regularly, but he was no youngster anymore.

Above the gusting rasp of the wind, he thought he heard a truck starting and pulling away. By the time he got to the higher ground and rounded the side of the slope to the top, he found no one there. He looked around. No shell casings either. He hadn't expected any. It had been a one-shot hit.

Still panting, he tugged out his cell phone and made the call. Then he started back. Fergie had already tied the boat to the dock and was standing beside where Bobby Ray had fallen.

Al stopped for a moment. The wind had let up. He looked around and listened. The air seemed strangely still, and he didn't see or hear a bird in any direction. Not a one.

"WHAT DO YOU THINK BOBBY Ray was calling you about?" Victor Kahlon, who had replaced Al as a sheriff's department detective, sat across the picnic table from Al and Fergie.

The silver Volvo station wagon of the medical examiner, Clive Barnes, was parked close. His slightly autistic assistant, Teddy, was stretching yellow tape around the scene. She had mousy brown hair and looked downward when focused on a task. Her stocky build along with the frown she often wore made her look tougher than she was. Al knew she had a secret fascination with movie celebrities and also a heart about as big as the state. She'd already come over to Al, interrupting Victor for a moment, to ask if Al or Fergie had brought along their dog, Tanner. When he said no, she showed a brief flicker of disappointment but had gone back to work. Tanner was like a therapy tonic for her. She got along far better with animals than people. Al had had moments in his long life when he felt the same way.

"I never got to find out. He wouldn't say." Al glanced over to where Clive was zipping up the body bag. "Did you find anything on him?"

"He had seven dollars in his wallet and little else except lint in his pockets. His car was mostly empty bottles and a funky smell that would give limburger a run for its money."

"He was supposed to know something," Al said. "He said it was life-or-death, for me to come ASAP to meet him at Muleshoe, and it couldn't wait."

"I guess it couldn't." Victor watched the crew lift the body bag to the stretcher.

Two other sheriff's department cruisers had their lights going, and a crime scene crew was looking over the distant area where a getaway vehicle might have parked.

"We have damn all little here, Al. Have you an idea about what this was about?"

"Not one."

"Bobby Ray came to the house a little over a week ago," Fergie said. "He gave Al his usual spiel about how he needed a place to stay, or he was going to be homeless. Al has known him for years. He'd let him stay at the house before."

"That was back when I lived there by myself," Al said. "Things are different now. Fergie and I just got married. As you know, my brother, Maury, his wife, Bonnie, and their baby live with us, as well as Patty Belle, who you promised to help with a citizenship lawyer and that summer session at the deaf school. I hated to turn Bobby Ray away, but it wasn't only my place this time."

Fergie put a hand on Al's forearm. "Tell him about the previous time."

"When I did let him stay at my place before, back in my living-alone days, he drank everything in the house except the cleaning products, and I'm not too sure about those. He constantly smoked cigarettes inside when I'd asked him not to, and he might have even stolen an item or two from around the house that he thought he could hock."

"His career has been on sort of a sideways skid," Victor said.

"He had his day, though," Al said. "Was a time I thought he was going to have his name up in the bright lights with the big boys. But then, you know."

"I sure do." Victor nodded. "I caught quite a few of his early shows. In his later days, he was working smaller venues and weaving his way back home. A few times, we found him sleeping in his car."

"I know." Al nodded. "He'd started on that path when I was still working for the department."

"Al even went to bat for him a couple of times, kept him from spending the night in jail," Fergie said. "Little good it did."

"But I didn't expect it all to end like this." Al watched the meat wagon haul away what was left of Bobby Ray. A department tow truck was hooking up his friend's car to take it for closer examination.

A couple of boats towing water-skiers sped by along the nearer shore, kicking up a couple of big wakes. Their radios were turned up, and the people inside the boats were whooping as loudly as they could. The woman skiing behind the second boat, either not knowing or not caring how sound carried over water, yelled, "This is way better than sex!"

Al's brother, Maury, could have provided a snappy comeback to that. But Al wasn't in the mood.

Coming up behind the boats were three jet skiers zigzagging among themselves, seeing who could get closest to the shore.

"Now, you're going to let us handle this, won't you, Al? Remember. You're retired now. You were out fishing. Why don't you just get back out there and catch a few bass," Victor said.

"We'll see," Al said. "We'll see."

Al narrowed his eyes, following the procession of vehicles leaving the park's ramp area.

Fergie gave his forearm a squeeze. She knew.

Chapter Two

Al passed through the front end of the Luckenbach Post Office—a general store at that end, full of T-shirts, bric-a-brac, and all manner of tourist goods—to enter the back end, a bar. In the corner to his right, two men in worn cowboy boots, jeans, and pearl-button shirts slouched in wooden chairs tilted back to rest against the wall.

One reached for a guitar leaning in the corner and passed it toward the other. "Why don't you lay down a few licks?"

The other man didn't put down his long-neck beer but just shook his head and said, "I'm more of a banjo sort of a guy."

Fergie, who'd been at Al's side, was already across the room at the bar, where a vest-wearing man in his late twenties or early thirties held up two long-neck bottles of Shiner Bock.

Al gave a short shake of his head.

Fergie leaned closer to the bartender, who switched out the beers for a couple of cans of Diet Coke.

Al stepped up to face the man putting the guitar back in the corner. "Did either of you two know Bobby Ray Champion?"

The man let go of the guitar, made sure it stayed in place, and turned with a tilted head to look up at Al. "I heared him play a few times 'round here and onced or twice in Fredericksburg. Good man, but you know. Wi-elt horses couldn't keep him from this stuff." He lifted his half-full beer toward Al, who didn't have to glance at his watch to know the time was only a little after ten in the morning. *Pot? Kettle?* Al shook his head. *It's not my call.*

Al could also never tell about the genuineness of all the bad grammar and Texas accents he'd heard. Sometimes he got "sell" for *sale*, "still" for *steal*, and he'd collected many versions of the word *oil*, from "ol" to "earl" to "oh-well." He also secretly believed that some folks were heavy-handed with all the twang just because they were partial to hearing themselves talk that way.

Neither of the men had commented on Al's use of the past tense when mentioning Bobby Ray.

Al sauntered over to stand beside Fergie.

"Jeff," the bartender introduced himself. "Heard you asking about Bobby Ray. A shame. A damned shame."

"You heard about it?" Al took a deep drink of soda, which was so cold it nearly gave him brain freeze, having just come out of a bath of ice cubes and melted water beside the necks of beer bottles sticking up in rows.

Jeff was looking up at Fergie, taking in her long red hair and the fact that she, at six-two, was taller than Al. "Radio said possible foul play. Surprised me."

"Why?"

"Ol' Bobby Ray was pretty used up. Bad health or even suicide wouldn't have surprised me none, though."

"Really?"

"He was old enough to be one of those fellows around when the rainbow only came in black and white."

"He was younger than me," Al said.

"Like I said." Jeff gave an eye roll and a hint of Elvis sneer that translated to a teenager's "Whatever."

Al glanced toward the tip jar but didn't reach for anything to put in. That wiped the look off Jeff's face. He leaned forward, his elbows on the bar. "Are you cops?"

"Retired," Al said. "She was a city detective. I was a county detective."

"But not this county, right?"

"Touché." Al shared his first grin.

"You think it was murder?" Jeff asked.

"A bullet in the back of the head is rarely suicide," Fergie said.

Jeff looked at her. "Sounds like it might be a drug deal gone bad."

"It was something gone bad," she agreed. "His last gig was here. Did you see him hanging around anyone? Or did anyone start anything that might be friction?"

"Not unless it was one of the staff. We liked Bobby Ray, and he could play and sing perty good, except his voice had gone to gravel. But he'd come to be a problem."

Al could guess what kind, but he waited. Half a dozen Harleys started up at once and took off in a low, rumbling roar. He imagined the string of tourists lined up to have their photos taken in the saddle on the back of Cowboy Bob's longhorn steer, Shot Gun. They would've turned their heads to watch the bikers heading off while kicking up a brown cloud of dust behind them.

"Couldn't fault him for being late," Jeff said when he could be heard. "He'd come early and stay late. But that was just so he could finish off every one of the courtesy beers we put in a cooler backstage for the bands."

"Did you notice him hanging out with anyone in particular?" Al asked.

"Nope. Truth be told, people had begun to kind of ease away from him. You know how it is. He'd lost the better part of that sparkle the ladies like. So he'd most often grab a couple of long necks on his break and head down to sit in the dry creek bed by himself."

"And when there was water in the creek?" Fergie bent her empty soda can in her hand and tossed it into the recycling bin.

"He'd sit on a stump on the shore and watch his hopes and dreams trickle by."

"You're a singer-songwriter too?"

"Tried. Friends told me all I had to do was put music to a few clichés. They were wrong. But give him his due—that Bobby Ray could write damn good lyrics and sing them, too, even when he was half in the bag."

"Were you friends?"

"I thought we were once. But you know..."

Al might have commented, but he kept it to himself. Everyone had a friend or two who they began to think of as a burden but with whom they were still friends.

"He wasn't staying out here?" Al asked.

"He did for a spell. I'd come in first thing in the morning and see him setting in the open door of his run-down car with a can of beer in one hand and a cigarette going in the other." Jeff shook his head. "But he rolled out of here not long back, probably so he could mooch off someone or crash at their place."

That someone had almost been Al... for a few moments, until he said no.

Al could remember that visit all too well, having replayed it enough times in his head during a largely sleepless night. Bobby Ray had shown up at Al's door, frowning when he heard a dog bark. He got even more downcast when he found out Al was married to Fergie and the down-stairs, where he'd stayed once before, was housing Al's brother, Maury, along with Bonnie; the baby, Little Al; and Patty Belle, a pale young deaf girl with a harelip and wispy blond hair, who'd joined their house-hold after they rescued her from some very bad people.

"I had a double reason for asking to stay here," Bobby Ray said. "I think someone might try to kill me."

"Really? Who?"

"Oh, it could be a whole lot of people. Someone wants me dead."

"And you think I might provide some protection?"

"You stood behind me in the past once or twice over the years."

Al figured he'd known Bobby Ray Champion for over forty years, going way back to the time he was new on the music scene and had the swagger of someone who just knew he was going to make it big. During a stretch there in the middle, Al wouldn't even get a wave from Bobby Ray when he was spotted in the crowd. But Bobby Ray had peaked early, and the downward spiral hadn't been nearly as pretty to watch. When he stood at Al's door, his voice a husky rasp and smelling like the floor of any number of saloons, he'd been about as far from up as he could get.

Still, he'd been a friend. Al had helped him before.

"I guess I might wind up being homeless." Bobby Ray had played that card before. He went back to his car after his most recent visit to Al, his head lowered.

That was the last Al had seen him, a friend who'd asked for help, and Al had turned him away.

"Don't let guilt eat you up," Fergie said as they emerged from the front door of the post office–gift shop–bar.

"I have a bad feeling about this," Al said. "That it's going to take more time and effort than I can imagine."

"Is it because of the snake? Do you think that was an omen?"

On their way to Luckenbach, they'd seen patches of blue along the highways, where bluebonnets would soon cover the ground in majestic waves of bright color. But the state had endured a mostly dry spring, and a drought had settled in throughout the state. Loose, dusty soil had drifted onto the small roads and even dimmed the color of flowers for stretches. They were on the long straight stretch, coming in the back way. A pickup truck ahead of them was kicking up white clouds of dust that roiled up in waves on either side of the narrow road.

Al slowed so that he wouldn't be driving through a cloud of dirt and end up arriving at Luckenbach looking like a powdered-sugar doughnut.

As the road cleared ahead, he sped up. As he approached the back of the truck, he saw its back wheel go over a line in the road. The line was a rattlesnake that had been zooming to cross the road in the heat.

The tire rolled over the snake, which arched its head and struck at the tire as the wheel cut it in half. Its fangs sank deep into the sidewall, and the stretch of the snake remaining behind the attached head flapped around and around as the truck drove on.

Al had to slow as the dust kicked up into a blinding cloud again. When they pulled into Luckenbach, he hadn't seen the truck parked anywhere. Later that day, the other driver would have to respond to a slow leak or just happen to glance down and see part of a rattler clinging to one tire. That wasn't going to be a happy moment.

Maybe it *had* been an omen. Al was already having a grumpy day. He'd been asked for help by a friend and hadn't helped, and the friend was dead. So no, the snake incident hadn't improved his mood one bit.

FERGIE WATCHED THE sprawl of Texas go by in yellow, brown, and green swaths outside the window as Al drove northward in the general direction of Austin. Occasional stretches along the sloping sides of the highway were taking on a bright-blue hue where the spring bluebonnets were farther along and had gotten the right amount of water and sun.

Standing at the corner of one ranch property they passed was a steel sculpture of a steer. Parts of its modern design were spaces open to the air, while others were covered in shiny chrome or blackened steel. Larger than real life, its horns swept out, and it seemed to be staring in the direction they were going. The damned thing had always puzzled her but not enough to inspire her to dig in and find out the story behind it.

"You know," she said, "Bobby Ray wasn't killed for his money, don't you?"

"He had none. Nor was it in some heated moment. It was deliberate and cold."

"Then it was for something he knew. He had a secret, one he might think he could cash in on, and knowing it got him killed."

"Probably."

"If we find who killed him, we'll also know the why. We'll know the secret too."

"That's likely."

"Then they will need to kill us too."

"They can try. Others have."

"It's not just the two of us I worry about," Fergie said. "There are six of us now, with your brother, Maury, Bonnie, Patty Belle, and Little Al in the house. We're all Quinns now, except maybe Patty Belle, and she's an honorary Quinn."

"You might as well throw in Tanner. A dog can be a Quinn too. Many have."

"I know how guilt can drive you."

"It's more than that. Should we stand by and let someone get away with just snuffing a person out? Any person? That's the sum of both our careers in law enforcement. We were among the ones who kept people from getting away with crimes like murder."

She nodded. "It is what we did. But now we're retired... and married."

"I know this is not much of a honeymoon. I haven't forgotten that we just barely got married."

"After a somewhat lengthy while."

"But we got there in the end."

She let out a hard huff of air. "Retired folks our age don't need honeymoons. They need good chairs and a chance to sit in them."

"You don't have to come along. I can do this on my own."

"No, you can't. If this is our honeymoon, then I'm going with you."

He looked at her and shared the first scrap of a smile she'd seen in a while. "I'll be glad to have you along for the ride."

As he spoke, his eyes tightened, and she caught him glancing into the rearview mirror more often than usual. He slowed to barely the speed limit and stayed in the right lane, letting other vehicles go around him in the fast lane.

She turned in her seat to peer behind them. After a second or two, she said, "The motorcycle?"

"Yeah."

"How long has it been following us?"

"All the way from Luckenbach, for all I know. He's on one of those fast little suckers and has been hanging back for quite a while. I tumbled to him because he's trying hard not to be seen."

"I noticed that too. How do you know it's a man?"

"Well, it could be one damn big chunk of a girl—one as tall as you and maybe twice your weight."

"You think I weigh only a hundred pounds or so? Well, bless your little pea-picking heart."

"Bonnie claims you're so skinny you can dodge raindrops."

"Well, isn't she sweet."

"I'm going to try something." Al signaled and pulled onto the highway's shoulder.

The ride had been quite peaceful, but as Fergie started to feel her heart beating, sitting still became harder. She watched as the motorcycle pulled onto the shoulder, too, a good way back.

After five minutes of waiting, Al shifted into gear and eased back into the flow of right-lane traffic.

The motorcycle pulled back onto the highway as well and kept its distance.

After a mile or two, Al pulled over again in a cat-and-mouse game that could have gone on for a while.

That time, the motorcycle swerved into the fast lane and accelerated into a roar as it whooshed past.

Al had to wait on a string of three slow-moving vehicles, then he pulled out and worked his way into the fast lane. The truck's engine rumbled as he put the gas pedal to the floor.

If Fergie thought her heart was thumping away before, she felt it really kick into high gear as Al wove in and out of traffic for the next few miles. She gripped the handle above the door as tightly as she could while Al kept the truck going as fast as it could, weaving from lane to lane like some drug-addled teenager.

But soon they realized they couldn't even see the black dot that had been the motorcycle. Al slowed at last and got into the right lane.

"I was hoping to at least get a plate number," he said. "But likely as not, it would've had mud rubbed across it. He was wearing a skull mask, too, so a facial ID was out of the question."

"I'm guessing you couldn't have caught up with him anyway," she said.

"Not likely, even with an Interceptor police cruiser's engine able to get up to a hundred thirty or even a hundred fifty. That was a Kawasaki Ninja and probably one of the high-end ones that can get to two hundred to two fifty."

"At least we know we stirred the pot," Fergie said. "Someone's interested in us now."

"I doubt that's a good thing."

"I hear you on that." She shook her head. "We don't know who or how many they are, but now they seem to know about us."

"What, oh, what have you gotten us into, Bobby Ray? Or maybe I should lay some of this on my sense of guilt," Al said. "But I've put some skin in the game now, and that extends to all of us, all the way from Maury to Tanner, from Bonnie to Little Al, and even to Patty Belle."

Chapter Three

Al had been driving steadily for two or three miles but hadn't said a word.

Fergie glanced at him. "Where are we off to now?"

"His last gig didn't give us much except to let someone know we were poking around about Bobby Ray. I doubt going back there would get us any more than we got, which was zip-a-dee-squat."

"So what, then?"

"Maybe we can learn more at his last port of call."

"*Cherchez la femme?*"

Al nodded. "He had two ex-wives. You'll be able to spot them. They'll be the ones square-dancing on his grave."

"Any girlfriends?"

"Kind of one."

"What do you mean?"

"You'll see."

"Give me a hint."

"Bobby Ray had what he called a groping groupie."

"He groped a woman?"

"More the other way around."

"She groped him?"

"Now you're getting warmer. Her name is Imogene Rachaels."

"That's her birth name?"

"I don't know. She went by 'I'm in Jeans' as a tomboy growing up. She has her own ranch these days—does all the roping and riding herself. No one dares call her Ima."

"Is she pretty?"

"I'll let you decide. He claimed she was a persistent fan at his gigs, and he'd successfully dodged her advances until he once got a little too drunk and woke up in her bed."

"Was that when he groped her?"

"More the other way around, like I said. He claimed she held him down, climbed on, and rode him like Paul Revere's horse."

"Oh my. You'd think that sort of thing would put him off drinking."

"Nothing could put him off drinking. Heaven knows that just about everything was tried, from rehab to tying him to a tree."

"That's the thing about gravity and a downward spiral," Fergie said.

At last, Al turned in to a narrow lane that led back quite a way to a small rustic wooden cabin of a house beside a far bigger stable. The stable, recently painted bright red, was in much better shape than the brown house.

They got out of the truck. A gust of wind kicked up a small pale-brown dust devil that swirled across their path as they walked to the front door. When they didn't see a doorbell, Al rapped his knuckles on the door, one covered with red paint that was chipping in spots, showing wood that the wind had sanded to a silvery hue.

No one answered. He knocked again.

The sound of hooves landing at a slow, deliberate pace came from the right side of the house, so Al and Fergie stepped around to see. Fergie figured the rider there had to be Imogene Rachaels. She was almost exactly like the portrait Fergie had been formulating in her head.

Imogene was wearing a fringed deerskin shirt over jeans and black cowgirl boots. On her head, she wore a white cowgirl hat with a rattlesnake-skin band. A couple of worn turkey feathers stuck up from one side, and the hat looked like it had seen long regular use, swatting away flying bugs as well as sheltering that tanned, weathered face from the sun.

"What can I do you folks for?" Her look wasn't all the way inviting. She probably had as many rascals coming out her way as people wanting to do business with her, assuming she was in some kind of business.

She was riding a huge black Percheron, a draft horse with feet like a Clydesdale's. The horse towered over them, weighed well over a ton, and was at least eighteen hands high.

"Her name is Muffin. It's okay to pet her a bit." Imogene reached down to pat the mare's neck. "She's mild-mannered and an absolute dream to ride."

Fergie stepped closer and ran a hand down the silky black nose. Muffin turned her head enough to fix one large, kind eye on Fergie, not a hint of malice or concern in it. A horse that size probably had a fair amount of self-confidence. Her huge nostrils twitched as she took a sniff and perhaps recorded Fergie's scent.

"You can follow me yonder. I've got to put the currycomb to her and love on her a little."

Imogene turned the mare and started off slowly enough toward the stable that they could follow without breaking into a run.

She led the horse inside, where in the dimmer light, Fergie could make out other horses in the stalls, some every bit as big as Muffin. The horses next to those seemed smaller, although they were full-sized. Fergie recognized a Morgan, having ridden one before. The stable smelled of straw, hay, and the not entirely disagreeable odor of horse droppings.

Imogene dismounted and loosened Muffin's cinch. She glanced up at Fergie, taking in the fact that she stood six feet two while Imogene herself was maybe five-five, including what the boots and cowboy hat gave her. She shook her head as she removed the tack to hang it all up on some of the few pegs still empty on the wall. She looked the horse over and even ran a hand under her belly after removing the saddle. She felt the mare's legs and went around to lift each leg to take a close look at the hoof and shoe. Then she reached for a currycomb and started in on the mare's black sheen of a hide. "Go ahead. Talking isn't gonna get in the way of anything. I shoe the horses myself, by the way. Even make the shoes myself. I'm a bit of a blacksmith as well as a trainer. Go on and jaw. Don't let me use up all the air around here."

Imogene was a stocky gal with a pouter pigeon chest. Fergie could imagine her shoeing the horses, as big as they were, lifting an anvil to carry it around, and getting the better of a drunken Bobby Ray in a tumble across the sheets. Try as she might, she couldn't stop herself from picturing the tall, lean Bobby Ray and the stout Imogene naked together in graphic detail, in a version of what Al had shared about those so-called romantic moments. A brief shudder rippled through her.

"You heard about what happened to Bobby Ray?" Al asked.

Imogene paused, lowered the currycomb, and reached up with a knuckle to rub at an eye, which had gone damp at the corners.

"Yes, I did. A helluva thing. I didn't expect that to be the what'd get him, but I figured something would."

"You two were pretty close?" Fergie asked.

"I don't mind telling you he had a thing for me."

"Well, he had a thing," Al said.

"Have you any idea who might have done something like this to him?" Fergie asked.

Imogene paused in her stroking and looked off through the open stable door to the brighter sunlight across the dirt of the corral. Her voice broke in a half-choking gasp. "Not a soul. He was a harmless dude, a talented singer, for my five cents, and he stayed completely away from anyone else's wife, and don't think they didn't swarm over him like bees on a hive back in those early days when he was climbing the rainbow on the up side."

"Lucky you were there sometimes to protect him," Al said.

"Damned straight."

Fergie looked away so Imogene couldn't see her suppressing a grin at Al being a bit of a smart-ass.

She had her face together when she turned back. Imogene had pulled down the mare's head and was looking into one of the ears.

"Well, what could it be?" Al asked. "Had Bobby Ray come across some club owner being crooked? Sometimes, that happens. A venue has fifty people in a crowd, and it turns into two fifty on the books so money from outside can come in and leave clean, taxes paid and everything. Places like that have been caught laundering before."

"I don't know if it was anything like that or if he witnessed a crime, maybe tripping over someone's Mary Jane patch. I guess anything's possible because he was kind of nosing around and talking to some shifty types."

"Like who?"

"Oh, a fair number of no-goodnicks. He had this thing, a jones, really, of late."

"Oh? Do tell," Fergie encouraged her.

Imogene sighed. "He told me once that 'with great risk comes great risk but sometimes a really sweet reward.' He made it sound like the beginning of a song he was writing in his head. He had gotten this notion about how to get back on top."

"What was that?"

"That a lot of the big, lasting country hits are about bad guys. You know, like Johnny Cash's 'I shot a man in Reno just to watch him die.' Hank Williams wrote a lot of songs like that, on the edge of crime. Bobby Ray was after that sort of thing, only somewhere else. Otherside-of-the-line stuff like 'Pancho and Lefty' as well as more eerie stuff like 'Ode to Billie Joe.' He had the first-hand experience, too, for something like Merle Haggard's 'The Bottle Let Me Down.'"

"So he wanted to venerate and somehow honor that sort of darkside-of-life stuff?" Fergie knew her eyes had snapped open wider, but she couldn't help that.

"Yeah, exactly. You know, like those Mexican singer-songwriters do with the cartels. They make folk songs that honor and glorify those gangsters. *Narcocorridos* are what Bobby Ray called that sort of music."

"You don't have any of his notebooks or anything he might have used to keep track of conversations he had with shady types?" Al had told Fergie he hadn't seen any in the rat's nest that was Bobby Ray's car.

"No. He didn't exactly do much songwriting here. He wasn't in the right frame of mind when he was here, and to be fair…" She gave a gruff cowgirl giggle. "I didn't give him much time for it."

As they were heading back out the long lane, leaving Imogene's spread, Al drove slowly, thoughtfully, while Fergie looked out the windshield and her window. Under a distant live oak, six zebras were standing in the shade of the tree's canopy. She blinked, thinking she was seeing things. But the zebras were still there.

Al's phone rang. He glanced at it as he tugged it out of his pocket and handed the phone to Fergie so he could stay focused on driving. "It's the home fires burning," he said.

"Oh?" She saw the call was from Bonnie.

"What's up?" Fergie asked. "Is anything the matter?"

Bonnie's voice shot up an octave higher than usual. "Al just got a package in the mail."

"And?" Fergie gave Al a raised eyebrow when he glanced her way with a question in his eyes.

"Can it wait?"

"You'd better let Al decide."

"Why?"

"Because the package is from Bobby Ray Champion."

Al didn't say anything, but he drove faster after Fergie handed the phone back and he put it away.

He went around a bend in the road a little too fast and had to touch the brakes before he could accelerate into the curve. His glance her way caught her staring at him. "What?"

"I was just trying to imagine how things would have turned out for you if you had gotten your way and lived alone through all your retirement years."

"Do you mean how did I come to be married? You beat me down with your good looks and your patience."

"Or how did you ever reconcile with Maury after he had an affair with your first wife after being best man at your wedding?"

"Not speaking to him for a good twenty years helped." Al glanced into the rearview mirror and saw no cop cars behind him, so he maintained his pace. "Maybe I stumbled onto a capacity to forgive. A bigger question is how did I come to have a small child in my house? Does that make me a grandfather type?"

"And a dog. You have a dog now, too, a rescued one."

"As for Tanner, I could kind of see that coming. I always wanted a dog, and now I have time to care for one."

Tanner was a small Australian cattle dog mix with bent ears and a tilted head. He'd taken in Al with careful eyes that didn't seem to expect much when they first met at a pet rescue center where human bones had been found in the incinerator. Tanner had been a day or two away from being euthanized because of his age and overcrowding. When Al took him home, Tanner had at first maintained a quite dignified reserve, not hoping for much and getting what he expected. Over time, he'd evolved into a loving and appreciative dog but one with a feisty side when he'd needed to defend Al or any of the others, which had happened more times than Al cared to mention.

"Having a dog is a good thing... when you're not gallivanting around Texas on one new mission or another," Fergie said. "But hey, I think having a family is an even better thing. It becomes you and has made you a warmer, more caring man. Taking in Patty Belle, an underage, illegally imported deaf girl is just one more sign of how far you've come toward being socially flexible when you could have been easing toward the rigidity of solitude."

"I'm not saying change has been a bad thing for me."

"But there's that one thing, isn't there?"

"Yep. It makes me vulnerable," he said. "Not that you're all some kind of kryptonite, just that someone can get to me through all of you."

"They've tried before," she said, "and they failed."

"But they haven't quit trying, and this time, I may have brought it on myself and all of you with trying to find out what's behind Bobby Ray's flat-out murder."

"I think you know that he was a spent bullet, a man on his way further down and out, and that law enforcement isn't going to pull out all the stops on his case the way you will."

"There is that." He didn't speak for the next few miles and just drove a little faster with each mile they got closer to their house.

Chapter Four

Bonnie and Patty Belle had finished washing and drying the dishes. As soon as she hung up her towel, Bonnie headed toward the package on the dining table as if it had a magnetic pull, glancing at Maury. He was standing by the front door with the living room curtain pulled aside, holding Little Al in his chest papoose. Tanner hovered at his feet, probably just as eager to see Al and Fergie as they were to get home.

Patty Belle looked around for something else to do, some sweeping, mopping, or cleaning up. Bonnie signed for her to have a seat at the table, but she started to dust instead. The household was trying to get across to her that she was no longer some sort of indentured servant, that she was a member of the family and could loaf around sometimes, like them.

She was deaf and unable to speak, but she could sometimes manage a little crackling giggle or silent knee-slapping laughter. At other times, she tried to hum or make an effort at off-tune singing, which, when loud, sounded like the exasperated honk of a large goose caught in a door. Her hum was heading that way until she saw Bonnie hold a finger up to her lips. So she went back to quietly dusting all the surfaces of the living area with a soft rag.

Bonnie picked up the bubble-wrapped manila package that had arrived in the mail for Al and worked on its seal with her fingernails.

"I thought you were going to let Al get home to open that," Maury said.

"I had the same trouble at Christmas. When I found wrapped packages under my mother's bed, I had to pick at them until I had them open. Then I became a master of wrapping them back up the way they had been. It was a chore acting surprised come Christmas morning, but I got pretty good at that as well."

"What's that sound?" Maury leaned closer to the front door to press his ear against it.

Tanner rose onto all fours and growled.

Bonnie had the end of the package open and peeped inside to see three black-and-white composition books. She slid one out and leafed through the pages. "I guess he was writing songs. Don't know why he'd send them to Al unless it was for safe keeping, and even that makes little sense."

"Do you hear that?" Maury's voice was so loud that the baby woke and waved his arms.

Bonnie cocked her head. "Oh my." She shoved the composition book back into the mailer and closed the end back up, using the sticky open ends to seal it. Then she dropped the package onto the table and started across the room.

"What?" Maury shouted, though he'd already started to follow her.

"That's a helicopter. You know that sound, and I'm betting it's no damned STAR Flight copter. These could be the cold stark opposite of people coming to help us."

She scurried downstairs. Patty Belle stayed as close to her as she could. First, Bonnie got her .38 Chiefs Special out from the stand beside their bed. Then she grabbed one of Maury's work handkerchiefs and wrapped it around Tanner's mouth to keep him from barking. He had shifted to a low, steady growl and was looking upward. She clipped on his leash.

She signed for Patty Belle to keep as quiet as she could, forgetting in her fretting that Patty Belle couldn't speak.

Maury stood at the bottom of the stairs, waiting to hear what she had in mind.

"Outside!" she snapped.

Patty Belle and Maury followed. He closed the door and screen quietly, though that hardly mattered as the roaring chop of helicopter blades lowered toward the ground in the nearest open area.

Bonnie couldn't think of anywhere to run where they couldn't be seen from the sky, so she ducked around the side of the house and tugged Tanner along as she opened the door to the small shed that housed the reverse-osmosis pump that brought the water up from the lake that Al used to use for all the house's water needs. He claimed it had sometimes made bath water brown, and he had used bottled water to brew coffee until he'd had a line of fresh water run to his house when all the other house construction was going on around him.

The inside of the windowless shed was dark. She could see spider-webs in the corners. As soon as the door closed behind them and they were in the near dark, with only a tiny sliver of light coming through here and there, she said, "You two get behind me and hold Tanner still. Squish in behind that old pump's tank. Even if they swing open the door for a look in here, they won't see you if you press close to the wall back there. Make sure Little Al has his binky too. I don't want a peep out of any of us."

Patty Belle tugged at Bonnie's arm, so Bonnie had to nudge the shed door open with one foot for long enough to sign the same thing to the girl, who nodded and moved closer to Maury so that she could put a hand on Little Al.

"What if they come in after us?" Maury wasn't able to suppress the tremor in his voice.

"Then I'll spray them full of more holes than a salt shaker."

IN THE DARK, PATTY Belle's shivering calmed as she patted the baby with one hand and Tanner's furry back with the other, all while pressing into Bonnie's soft, roundish side. Even while hiding, as they were, she felt safer than she had as one of eight fatherless children in the Philippines. She was with people who leaped in and did things. They'd saved her when the promises of others had been lies. She'd looked into mirrors and knew she wasn't pretty, but she'd still fallen for the lies that she would have a wonderful job and a life in America. Instead, she'd ended up as an unpaid servant in a brothel—not attractive enough to be turning tricks as the others her age or even younger were doing.

Sounds inside the house could mean someone was coming or going. She pressed harder against Bonnie and tried to remember to breathe.

AL AND FERGIE WERE nearly home. He drove at borderline-reckless speeds, sliding on turns and spraying gravel when a wheel slipped off the asphalt onto the road's shoulder.

"Seems only last week you were beefing about the most recent residents of all the newly built houses being the ones shooting out of their drives like Indy or Daytona cars," Fergie said.

Al didn't respond but just pressed his lips tighter together and stamped down harder on the gas.

He heard the sound before he saw a black Sikorsky S-76 helicopter rising from the road ahead of them and taking off. It wasn't like any of the black-ops copters he'd seen in action before. It was a private limousine of the air and possibly up to no good.

He reached for his glove box as he drove. His Glock was in there.

But the Sikorsky spun and rocketed away with a roar.

Al put his right hand back on the steering wheel.

"Were you thinking of sliding to a stop, hopping out your door, and unloading a clip at it?" Fergie asked.

"I saw only a few figures through the windows. None of them looked like any of our folks, Maury or Bonnie."

"Oh, Al. I have a very bad feeling about this."

Al rushed the truck down the lane to his house, where Fergie's car was parked out front.

As soon as he was stopped, he grabbed the Glock, scooted out his door, and ran to the house. Fergie was ahead of him and swung the front door open. He rushed inside, covering every corner, and checked the bedrooms, the bathrooms, and the closets upstairs as well as down.

The inside of the house was preternaturally still, with only a light breeze coming through the screen door to the balcony on the upper floor. None of them were there, not even Tanner.

"Clear!" he called out to her.

Fergie came in and went right to the master bedroom to get Al's Sig Sauer out of the drawer of the bedside table. She came back into the living area with the gun hanging in her right hand. "Where is everyone? Do you think someone took them away?"

"I sure didn't see them in the copter. Think," he said. "Think like Bonnie would."

"Outside," Fergie said. "If they're here, they'll be hunkered down somewhere outside. She was raised by her dad to hunt outdoors, and her first impulse would be to get there."

They both went downstairs for one more quick look around the space where Maury, Bonnie, and the baby stayed. *Nothing.* Patty Belle had been sleeping on the living room couch, and she hadn't been there or anywhere upstairs.

As they went out the back door, they looked around. Al could see nothing from there, nor did he expect to. The fishing dock and the dock where his boat had been raised on its electric winch were too wide open. The others had to be someplace close, where they could hide quickly.

"Ah." Al waved a hand and started around to the side of the house. Fergie followed.

EVEN THOUGH SHE COULD be pretty fearless for her own sake, Bonnie quivered in her skin the whole time she and the others were cowering in the dark, listening to heavy footsteps thudding through the house. The only light coming in was from tiny cracks and an occasional pinhole, not enough for them to even see each other.

The old pump room felt dank and moldy. She tried not to think of the spiders, roaches, or even scorpions that might have been crawling around them. The more she tried not to think of them, the more she could imagine their little legs clicking across the hard floor and walls as they came toward her. She reached to sweep an imaginary bug off Little Al's head and found Patty Belle's hand already there, doing the same thing.

Every time Tanner's growl got louder, and she had to put a hand down to calm and quiet him, or when Little Al stirred and began to make a noise before Maury could ensure his binky was in place, she felt like all the blood was running out of her, leaving her in an icy chill.

When at last they heard the footsteps leaving the house, followed by the chopping roar of the helicopter rising and whooshing away, Bonnie held the others still, waiting, listening. Maury had whispered in her ear that they could leave their hiding hole, but then she heard steps again, less like booted thuds, but they were steps.

She whispered back, "We stay."

They waited for what seemed hours more.

Then Bonnie heard the downstairs back door open and close. "Uh-oh."

Steps came their way around the back corner of the house. She lifted the Chief's Special and pulled the hammer back in a series of clicks that seemed way too loud.

The doorknob turned slowly, and light flooded the room as the door opened, letting the bright outside in.

Her finger was tightening on the trigger when she heard Tanner's happy whine from behind his bandana muzzle and felt his tail slapping against her leg as he lunged toward the door.

She lowered the pistol.

Outside the door stood Al and Fergie.

Bonnie yanked the makeshift muzzle off Tanner and rushed forward to throw her arms around Fergie in a hug, always a challenge since she was around five feet three and Fergie was six-two. Patty Belle's eyes were still open wide in fear. She was only slowly making the shift to joy.

Maury came out into the daylight and managed a sideways arm around Al's shoulders, managing not to crush the chest papoose containing Little Al between them. "We're sure glad to see you guys."

Tanner first jumped up on Al's legs then bounded over to give Fergie some of the same welcoming attention.

Bonnie blinked, looking around. The outdoors sure seemed bright after having been in that hole so long, though she doubted the scare from the intruders had lasted even twenty minutes.

"Did you get a look at those guys?" Fergie asked as they all went inside and up the stairs to the living area.

Since the house was built on the steep pitch of a hill, both front and bottom-level doors opened onto lawns.

"Nope." Bonnie glanced at Maury.

He shook his head.

"Look around. See what's missing," Al said. "That sort of popping in and out doesn't make any sense unless they were after something, and they must have found it, or they would have kept looking and maybe discovered you guys."

Bonnie unleashed Tanner and scurried back down the stairs. Maury looked around the living area while Little Al slept on, his head resting against Maury's chest. Tanner sniffed a path to the front door then around the room until he came to the dining table. He stopped there.

When Bonnie came back upstairs, she said, "Nothing missing down there, though it wouldn't have broken my heart if they had made off with some dirty diapers."

Al and Fergie were just coming out of the master bedroom. "Nothing missing in there." He nodded toward the Sig Sauer Fergie was holding at her side in one hand. "They didn't even take that."

Bonnie stared at Tanner, then her eyes swept the table's surface.

"It's gone!"

"What's gone?" Fergie asked.

"The package Al got from Bobby Ray. It was lying right there on the table."

"That's all they took?" Al asked.

"Must've been all they wanted. What they were after," Bonnie said.

Chapter Five

While Maury took Little Al downstairs to put him in his crib, Bonnie started a pot of coffee. Patty Belle had to stand on tiptoe to get down some mugs. Al and Fergie both slipped back outside.

Fergie checked to make sure they'd closed the doors to the truck. They walked all the way around the house and saw nothing other than some boot prints. She bent closer to see mashed grass for a short stretch in the direction where the copter had alighted.

Once back inside, Fergie sat down at the dining table.

"I wish to hell I knew what was in that package"—Al stood by the windows facing the lake, looking out across the slight ripples—"or how they knew Bobby Ray might have sent something to me."

"Well, um, I kind of peeked a little before they made off with the package." Bonnie carried two steaming mugs over to the table and slid them in front of Fergie and in front of an empty seat for Al.

She went back to the stove to get two more mugs for Maury and herself. He was just coming up the stairs, wiping his hands with a towel. "If anyone had told me that in my golden years, I would be changing diapers, I would have knocked them apex over apple cores regardless of their age or sex."

"Really? You looked?" Fergie ignored Maury and stared at Bonnie. "What was in there?"

Bonnie plopped down into a chair and took a sip of her coffee first. Then she spoke over the lifted rim of the mug. "I know I shouldn't have. The package was addressed to Al. It was a manila bubble wrap package, addressed by hand, and inside were three of those black-and-white composition books like we used to use in school."

"What was written inside?" Al picked up his steaming mug and carried it over to stand by the windows.

"I only looked at one—glanced, really. But it looked like he was writing songs. I wonder why he'd bother to send them to you."

"I'm wondering that myself." Al tilted his head, listening.

Fergie heard it, too, a growing roar coming their way.

Al shook his head. "Just a boat."

But they were all a little twitchy and on edge.

"Do you remember any of it?" Fergie turned back to Bonnie. "A squeeze of his suggested he was trying to write some crime-related songs to give them extra buzz in the biz."

"He was squeezing someone?" Maury asked.

"More the other way around." Fergie stayed fixed on Bonnie. "Well?"

"I just flipped through the pages a little. Some words were crossed out, and arrows went here and there. He'd made some notes about keys or chords in the margins. It sure seemed like some sort of a song coming together, crawling itself into life on the page."

"Do you remember any of the words?" Al put his mug down on the table and leaned closer.

"I recall Port Dexter was mentioned a couple of times, but that's mostly all I remember—oh, and that it wasn't about Mary Jane or Columbian marching powder. I figured out what he was going for there, but I guess it wasn't what the song was about. Though I'll be damned if I came away knowing what that tune *was* about."

"Port Dexter is down along the Gulf Coast, somewhere between Port Aransas and Port Arthur, isn't it?" Maury asked.

Al nodded. "It's just another shrimp boaters' port, for all I've heard, and it's nothing like the touristy spots."

Fergie stared down into her emptied coffee mug. "There must be something about it that Bobby Ray thought was song-worthy."

"Are you going to saunter down that way and have a look around?" Maury asked.

"I may have to. But I'm not comfortable leaving you, Bonnie, Patty Belle, and the baby here. Tanner as well."

"Why?"

"Someone has proven they can pretty much waltz in and take what they want," Al said. "You're not safe here. None of you are."

At another roar of a motor coming their way, Al stood and went back to the window. "A plane this time." He shook his head. "Any one of us staying here would be twitchier than a long-tailed cat in a room full of rocking chairs, as Tennessee Ernie Ford used to say."

"We can't stay?" Bonnie looked around the room and ended on the fridge, which she'd just stocked.

"You would have to be on your toes all the time if you stayed here. A sniper shooting along with a copter that looked too much like the kind mercenaries use make me think someone might change their minds about just leaving us be."

"A road trip?" Maury asked, his voice only half as enthusiastic as he was trying to be. "Oh frabjous joy!"

"Oh man." Bonnie frowned. "Patty Belle was supposed to go away for her summer camp thingie in a couple of weeks."

Victor Kahlon, who held the detective position at the sheriff's department, which Al once had, was working with them to arrange an immigration lawyer. Though Patty Belle and Bonnie could communicate via American Sign Language, she still had a number of things to learn if she was to become an American citizen, so she was scheduled for a brief summer orientation camp at the Texas School for the Deaf to round out her social skills.

Bonnie's hands moved briskly as she signed to let Patty Belle know what was going on.

Then Bonnie shook her head again and went off to pack as little as possible since it would be a carload. Patty Belle had little to pack but looked more eager than sad to be traveling.

Fergie could see something in Al's eyes as he got up from the table and headed toward the master bedroom. She finished the rest of her coffee and took the mug over to the sink to give him a moment or two. Then she followed.

When she came into the room, he had the gun safe open and was taking out his small duffel bag of tricks and some extra boxes of 9mm ammo.

He turned and took in her raised eyebrows. "I may have really stepped in it this time."

"I think you were screwed either way, whether you took him in or let him spin on his own. He's the one that, for some reason, chose to tangle you up in the mess he was making."

He shrugged.

"You don't think it's drugs, do you?"

He shook his head. "You've dealt with Columbians in the past and some of the cartel bunches that can be as bad. They hit with a scorched-earth intensity, killing the whole family, the pets, the grass on the lawn... and then they burn down the house. This place would be just a scorched hole in the ground if that's what this is about."

"Well, it's about something, enough for Bobby Ray to be taken out by an experienced sniper and then have the next thing to black ops land near your house."

"No. I don't like it, not one bit. But we can't sit here and hope they don't come back to finish cleaning up. Whoever is in charge may decide someone peeked at those singer-songwriter notes and send a crew back to try to erase us."

"And you're planning something like a preemptive strike?"

"Something like that." He got his Sig Sauer out of the bedside table's drawer and put that in the bag too. "At least nose around, see if anything is going on, and we can't leave the others behind, dammit."

"Why don't we lock the bedroom door and take a few minutes?" She glanced toward the bed.

"Really?"

"It might calm you down a bit."

"Well... You're usually right about these things." He grinned and lowered the bag to the floor.

After a while, Tanner, who did not like to be locked out of their room, came and scratched at the door. They ignored him.

Chapter Six

The last few miles of Fergie's driving to Port Dexter took them along the coast for a stretch. Al tried to enjoy catching occasional glimpses of water past a collection of coastal businesses and buildings that got scruffier the closer they got to the city. He'd always enjoyed the smell of salt water and the sound of waves lapping the shore. But all he could see at the moment were foreboding shadows. Something was going on in those parts, and it had gotten Bobby Ray killed. Whatever was going on wasn't likely to ignore Al and his quirky little family unit.

"You've been in a remarkably calm and mellow mood on this trip so far," Maury said from the back seat.

Al glanced at Fergie. They'd taken her car so that the baby seat could fit between Bonnie and Maury, with Patty Belle crowded in. Fergie would know he hadn't been nearly as calm as Maury thought, more pensive than relaxed.

Tanner was crouched at Al's feet, though from time to time, he squirmed up to look out the side window or tried to get up to its slightly open top to sniff at the air rushing in.

The whole way, from leaving the rolling up and down of Texas Hill Country, to skirting the towering stone and glass of San Antonio in the distance, and finally to traversing the flatter former seabeds near the coast, Al had been mulling over his life. He'd expected to live out his days single and savoring solitude, fishing, taking walks, and playing chess with himself. Instead, he was married and in a crowded car with his once-estranged brother, Maury, their two wives, his dog, Patty Belle, and the baby, Little Al.

"What are you shaking your head at?" Fergie asked.

"Oh, just reminiscing."

They were passing the outside fringe buildings of Port Dexter. Thicker clusters of buildings lined the main through street ahead of and around them. Al had an initial impression that left a bad taste of wariness in his mouth. Although the sun was shining, he felt rather than saw a sense of grayness wherever he looked. The buildings appeared tired, faded, and worn—not the bright, sparkling welcome of a coastal town. Only one or two people were on the sidewalks, moving quickly and looking like they didn't want to be there. The only flag he could see was tattered and hanging limp on its pole with an occasional upward flutter, only to collapse again. Even a dog that came out of an alley and turned to go back in had its tail down and gazed around with wary eyes.

A wooden walkway leading to a fishing pier was boarded over and marked Closed.

As Fergie drove through the business heart of the town, only an occasional person hurried across the street ahead of them, their glances furtive. Motels and more bars than usual crowded the gas stations and convenience stores. Al saw none of the gift shops and typical markers of a touristy coastal town.

A crumpled yellow page of a newspaper rolled across the street like a tumbleweed.

"It's no Port Aransas," Maury said.

"Nope," Bonnie agreed. "No pirate ship, boogie board rental place, or signs pointing toward a bird sanctuary."

"I suspect any birds have flown the coops of this town." Maury must have been getting the same sensation Al felt.

Fergie was also picking up on whatever seemed a little off. She slowed and looked down the side streets with care.

They hadn't talked about what they would do if they did find something amiss in the town, nor did they expect that whatever might be going on would be blatant or obvious.

At the end of the town, where businesses thinned out again, Fergie turned the car around and went back through. Al saw no signs for fishing guides or charter boats, and the bars they passed again didn't advertise live music. Even more ominous, though it was late in the afternoon, he saw one shrimp boat heading out while another was coming in.

"You've been to shrimping towns before, Maury. What time do the shrimpers go out and come back?"

"The ones I've seen in action are usually heading out at sunset and coming back in around dawn. Or some go out at dawn. Still others, the big ones, go out for thirty to forty days at a time, freezing their catch. But they don't usually go in and out at varied hours."

"You think something smells fishy?" Fergie asked.

"Yeah, and it's not shrimp. Why don't we take a quick drive over to the beach before we look around?" Al knew he was letting his preconceptions of the town take over. He needed to clear his head and be as objective as possible. He couldn't just look around a place and sniff out crime and corruption.

He supposed some people were drawn to mountains, and he'd met one or two who craved wide-open spaces, even deserts. But for him, the sound and smell of ocean waves always soothed him and recharged his batteries as much as anything.

Fergie wove her car through the maze of warehouses and ramshackle houses until the streets played out along a row of parking spaces next to a greenish-brown dune.

They got out of the car, always a production with a child, Patty Belle, Al's dog, and four adults. Once out, they started along a path to the shore.

Al's gasp left his mouth hanging open. Fergie reached out to hold his hand, knowing the environmental slap in the face he was feeling.

The once-sandy beaches were densely sprinkled with litter as far as Al could see in either direction. Much of the debris was plastic, but he could also see medical waste: blood vials, syringes, IV pouches, and even diabetic lancets.

They stopped by the remains of a park bench that had been underwater more than once. One end tilted down toward the dirty sand. A wrinkled gray blanket rose at one end, and a head covered in a gray-white beard and tousled hair looked at them with squinting blue eyes.

"You'd best not go barefoot," the man cautioned them in a creaky voice. "Folks claim you can get AIDS from stepping on shared drug needles sticking up in the sand."

He lowered his head back to the tilted bench and pulled the blanket back over it.

No, this is not turning out to be a good day at the beach.

Tanner wanted to race across the beach to have a go at some gulls swooping down at the edge of the waves lapping the shore. Even they were avoiding landing amid the clutter of plastic and waste. Al kept a tight grip on the leash so that Tanner couldn't run.

"Let's not stay here looking at this." Fergie gave Al's hand a tug.

He turned and let her lead him back to the car. Neither Maury nor Bonnie had said a thing. They seemed to sense the broken glass in Al's gut at seeing nature so violated. Bonnie was holding Little Al tighter to her chest.

"Uh-oh." Maury pointed ahead.

A police cruiser was pulling up behind Fergie's car. Two cops got out of the car and started toward them.

Fergie shook her head. "An already-perfect day taking an uglier turn?"

"What fresh hell...?" Maury started to say but stopped when he saw the bigger bull of a cop glaring at them. The smaller cop, with the face of a weasel and a wry twist to his mouth, seemed to be thinking up something clever to say.

"What are you people up to?" the big cop asked.

As they got closer, Al took in a face with squinty eyes and the reddened skin of a hard drinker, always a good feature in a cop. His dark-blue uniform bulged—mostly from fat but probably a good bit of muscle too. He looked like a high school football lineman whose fitness was slowly ebbing but wasn't all gone just yet.

"Is this the way you always greet tourists who come to see your town?" Fergie asked.

The big cop was tall enough to look down at Fergie a little.

"You ain't the usual sort of tourists we get," the weasel said. The nameplate on his chest read Adams. His eyes swept over them, ending up fixed on Patty Belle.

The bigger cop's nameplate read Mendlemann. He glared at his partner. Fergie frowned at his squint behind clear aviator glasses and the way he chewed gum with his mouth partially open.

The shorter cop had to be five feet five or five feet six, tops. He looked up at Fergie. "Did you play basketball?"

She glowered down at him. "Did you play miniature golf?"

Adams's little body seemed to be trying to climb inside out as he quivered with a suppressed rage that turned his face pink then a darker red that rose all the way to his temples.

The bigger cop turned to stare at Al. "It would probably be best if you moved on. There are plenty of good places to vacation up and down the coast."

"A bus is leaving town—be under it?" Maury asked. He tried to add a chuckle to spin it as a joke.

The deadpan looks the cops gave him in return said it wasn't a time to be jolly.

"Are the local businesses okay with tourists being turned away?" Al asked.

"They're fine, just fine with it," Mendlemann said, his voice a scruffy growl, his eyes narrowing into a tighter squint.

"Okay, then." Al steered Fergie around one side of the two cops. He had to reach down to calm Tanner, whose ears and hair on his back said he was on full alert. A low growl had started in his throat.

Bonnie, Maury, and Patty Belle went around the other side of the cops and got quietly into the back seat.

"Way to go about getting along," Al murmured to Fergie as he slid into the passenger seat.

"Well, he walked right into that one," she said. "I just had to truck out that old saw after that. And just when have you ever seen a real cop that height?"

"What do you mean?" Maury asked from the back seat.

"That they neither looked like nor comported themselves as the kind of men who ever went to a police academy," Al said. "On the other hand, they showed remarkable restraint for the kind of hired thugs we think they are, something Fergie was testing perhaps a little incautiously."

The cops were heading back to their cruiser as Fergie pulled away. She was almost certain they'd copied down her plate number.

"Not cops, eh?" Maury said. "Well, they weren't community theater material either. Usually, it's the little one who's the smart one but not this time."

Al turned to glance behind them. "Anyone else feel like we're off to an ominous start here?"

Chapter Seven

"Aren't we headed the wrong way?" Maury looked out the back window at the outlying buildings of Port Dexter growing smaller behind them. "I thought you were going to look around and figure out what's going on."

"Tell him, Fergie," Al said.

She kept her eyes on the road. "We've already seen sniper work. You had a visit from... We might as well call them black ops. Then the minute we get to this cozy coastal town that should be rolling out the red carpet to tourists, we get a 'move along' nudge from a couple of... If they're real cops, I'll eat Al's fishing cap, sweatband and all."

"I just want to go home." Bonnie's voice had gone squeaky and thin. "To *our* home. How did this happen, that we end up roaming around like nomadic gypsies?"

Maury reached across Patty Belle and the sleeping baby to pat her shoulder. "Apparently, my brother, Al, is a giver, the sort that attracts the likes of a taker like Bobby Ray Champion. Al said no this time, but then Bobby Ray's screwed-up karma reached out to take away our comfort and freedom."

"But how can you fix this?" Bonnie's voice was definitely a whine.

"I don't know yet," Al said.

"We're going to have to know a lot more than we do now," Fergie said.

THEY PULLED INTO THE Aransas Pass Enterprise car rental agency moments before it closed for the day at six o'clock.

While they switched out all their stuff into the rental, Bonnie kept asking, "Why? Why? Why?" She expected no answer but was stuck on the idea. "Everything's happening so fast."

Fergie drove her car into the storage unit then put a shiny new padlock on the door and entered Little Al's birthdate as the combination.

Little Al squirmed in Bonnie's arms, perhaps picking up on her restless discomfort as Fergie drove until they found a motel with a vacancy.

"Do you really think all these steps are necessary?" Bonnie asked.

"Absolutely," Al said. "I'd send you off to another state if I could."

Bonnie stayed quiet, holding Little Al close to her chest until Maury came out of the motel's office and held up a thumb. They had two rooms, and the place was dog friendly. She let out a long, elaborate sigh and climbed out of the car then watched Al and Fergie drive away, headed back toward Port Dexter. She wanted to say she hoped that wouldn't be the last she ever saw of them. Maury came over and put a hand on her shoulder before reaching to pick up their bags.

When they were settled at last, the sun was fading on the western horizon to their right as they looked across the waves from their motel room. At the sound of a tap on the door, Maury went over to let in the elderly female manager who was pushing a collapsed crib on wheels.

"There's a rollaway bed just outside for the young lady." She nodded toward Patty Belle.

Tanner lifted his head from where it hung down where he was sprawled on the room's couch. Lately, he'd been sleeping like that, his head hanging down like some kind of Salvador Dali clock. He hopped down to trot over to the door.

"Here, let me give you a hand with that," Maury said.

"Thanks. I'm Mary Doughrety." She reached the back of one hand down for Tanner to sniff. "You all were lucky to get the last two rooms I got."

"I don't know why we didn't just stay in Port Dexter," Bonnie said.

"Oh, by gum, you shouldn't do that."

"Why?"

"I can't say. Just don't."

"What's so damned mysterious about that place?" Maury popped the crib open and spread the sheets and blankets over the mattress.

"I used to have a motel there. I got moved on but was darn near given this place, so I can't squawk nor talk about it none. I already said too much. You folks get settled in now." She paused at the door and turned to look at Maury. "If I didn't know better, I'd say you were a baby boomer like me."

"I am," he said.

"Well?" She nodded toward the much younger Bonnie and the baby.

Maury grinned. "Want to hear my theory about the baby boom?"

Bonnie groaned. Little Al reached a hand toward her mouth.

"You see, most young folks don't know much about baby boomers or even why there was a baby boom. Theirs is a generation that never used a dial phone in a booth or were ever given a spoonful of castor oil as a parental punishment."

"My mom used cod liver oil." Mary tucked away a stray lock of dyed-blond hair that had probably been white.

"It's hard for youngsters these days to envision a time in which the number-one locale from which to purchase condoms was a machine in the men's room of a gas station. Usually, some clever wag had graffiti-written on the side of the machine such wit as 'Don't chew this gum. It tastes like rubber.' Or 'Bust one. Win a baby.' The cost of the condom was usually a quarter, the same price as a beer or a shot of bourbon. It became something of a war of commodity choices, and in such battles, alcohol often wins. So that right there is one theory that explains the baby boom."

Bonnie let out a loud sigh.

Mary bent to give Tanner another pat on the head. When she stood up straight, she winked at Bonnie. "So it wasn't his wisdom and silver tongue that wooed you, eh?"

Then she bustled out the door.

"THERE'S NO GRACEFUL way out of this now, is there?" Fergie was looking out the passenger window as they approached the growing glow that formed an aura over Port Dexter.

"Nope. We need to fix this and expose whatever's going on, if we're ever to live free again."

"They are very good and hyperprofessional, or someone would have tumbled to their thing, whatever that may be. They've stayed small, focused, and are probably making enough money to keep at it and protect it."

"All because Bobby Ray Champion wanted to put some edge to his songs."

"You've got to admit his songs needed something. You recall his highest climb onto any charts was with:

Every moonbeam breaks a heart.

Paints icicles with its art,

Lights the wave tips on the sea,

But never brings you back to me."

"Yeah, he needed something. That's for sure. Not like Luke Spangle when he got married, and his songs lost so much edge everyone said his new stuff was like daisies coming out his ass. Bobby Ray had sure been writing some certifiable sop lately. He needed a jolt of a change. But I just wish to hell he'd kept us out of the picture." Al glanced at Fergie.

Without makeup and with enough eye shadow applied on her lower face to give her a five-o'clock shadow, she still looked pretty hot. She wore one of his shirts over her jeans and had her long red hair tucked inside a ball cap.

"Do you think I'll pass for a dude?" she asked.

"If the bar lights are dim enough. And I suspect they will be."

"Maybe everyone will be focused on the younger ones in the crowd."

"Let's not think of ourselves as old," Al said, "but as just not particularly youthful, or we'll both remind ourselves that we're getting too old to be doing this sort of tomfoolishness."

"Whoo-ee. I'll second that," she said. "When I warm up for a jog these days, my joints sound like a popcorn machine getting started."

"Let's hope we don't have to do any running tonight."

He slowed the rental car and looked over the array of gaudy neon names like The Bent Fox's Tail, Gnarly Gus, and Bayou Bunny. Of those, the bunny one stood out by having the most lights and being located next to an adjacent—perhaps even connected—motel.

A middle-aged man got out of his truck and scurried across the street, glancing from side to side as though trying not to be seen as he pushed inside the bunny bar.

Al glanced at his watch, which read ten o'clock. "It's early times, but let's start there."

He parked in an empty space half a block away. As they walked toward the bar's door, he noticed that Fergie had picked up a man's strolling gait. She would do fine, he thought, if the lights were dim.

Not only were the lights dim, but a layer of cigarette smoke formed a chest-high cloud they had to wade through to get to a corner table. Fergie slid her chair back so she could sit in the shadiest spot.

They had barely settled when a young girl, Filipina or some other kind of Asian, came over and asked, "Do you want company?"

Al shook his head. The girl faded back into the haze of smoke.

A Latina girl appeared next. "Wanna party?"

As she left, Fergie said, "Getting our drink orders doesn't seem to be priority one here."

Above the clinking of glasses and the low murmur of conversations, country and sometimes rock music played, just loud enough to turn the overall sound in the room into a blur of white noise.

Every table had an ashtray with a book of matches in it. The place was a little loosey-goosey on the indoor-smoking laws that existed elsewhere, making it feel like a blast from the past. Al picked up the matchbook and slipped it into his pocket.

A waitress finally made her way to their table. She was twice the age of the other roaming girls, who looked to be in their early twenties or even younger.

Al ordered a scotch and soda and Fergie a rum and coke, both drinks they could spill to one side when they got a chance, even though they'd paid three times the normal price.

Just about every seat at the tables and the bar slowly filled, though one of the young women occasionally led a customer off to the hallway leading back to the restrooms.

The clientele was almost all male, some men by themselves, others in noisier groups of two or three. The next time one of the girls led a man toward the hallway, Al got up and went to the men's room. Just as he entered the hallway, the girl opened a door at the end of the hall, past the restroom doors, and led the man out. Al turned around and went back to the table.

He nodded to Fergie. She rose, and they wove through the room to the front door. Once outside, they waited until they were back inside the rental car to talk.

"The motel next door, right?" she asked.

"Yep."

"I think we know how that one works," Fergie said. "Let's take a look at one or two more."

The next two night spots they entered along the main street were variations on the first, though in one case, the motel was across the street, and a young woman was leading a man to it as they pulled up.

"I've been in many a bar in my day," Fergie said as they left the third one, "though not as smoky as these for quite a while. But they were singles bars, what we called 'meat market' bars. Nothing as blatant as what we've seen was taking place."

Beneath the usual hum of music, conversations, and the clink of drinks being mixed or glasses cleaned, Al had picked up on an antic, almost frantic mission of quick connections being made. They'd each been propositioned at least half a dozen times in each place.

Al turned the rental car onto a side street and drove for a couple of blocks before he spotted anything like an open business. The streetlights were fewer and dimmer, so the lights of a tavern drew them like moths to a flame. The sign said Floy's Place.

Barely inside the door, Fergie leaned closer to whisper, "Now *this* is different."

First of all, Al could smell food—real, well-cooked food. The lights were bright, and the arrangement looked more like a diner than a bar, although most of the patrons had a beer in front of them as well as bowls of what looked like hearty stew.

They slid into a booth with red Naugahyde seats crowding a Formica table. The fry cook himself came out around the counter to take their order, which didn't take long since only half a dozen options were chalked onto a blackboard of a menu. The black cook, another former football-lineman-sized man, had the splatter of varied sauces on his once-white apron with "Floy" embroidered in red thread. Some of his former muscle had settled at his waist into a belly, and he looked to be running the place on his own, which kept him moving about briskly. He barely looked at them as he rushed back to his grill.

Al's BLT and Fergie's tomato soup were brought out only a few minutes later. The cook had thrown in a grilled-cheese sandwich with

Fergie's soup. "Because that's the way people should eat tomato soup," he said.

She slid her sandwiches over to Al as soon as the cook was back behind his counter.

The cook's roundish build, the stubble on his cheeks and chin, and the fact that he was losing his hair fit the stereotype of a cook in an all-night joint so closely that Al doubted he could've described the man or picked him out of a lineup the next day.

The interesting thing, though, was how a large portion of the clientele got up from their meals at the same time and headed out the door.

"Think they're working some sort of night shift?" Fergie asked.

"Looks that way to me." Al paid their tab without seeming in too great a hurry, and they went out into the night.

All the men who'd just left Floy's headed in the same direction. Al and Fergie slid into the rental and followed at a distance. When the men entered a warehouse-sized building half a block away, Al pulled over and turned off his lights.

Aside from the light of the small door opening and closing, the building was dark.

Al was about to slip out and go have a look around when a double-wide garage door opened, showing a wide-open brightly lit area where men were working on cars, mostly pulling them apart. A car that had been coming down the street turned and went inside. The door closed again, and the building was dark once more.

"Well?" Al asked.

"Sure looked like a chop shop to me. I wonder where they get all the vehicles. Do you suppose some come from as far away as Houston?"

Before Al could answer, a car eased up behind theirs, and red and blue lights began to swirl.

"Well, this can't be good," Fergie said.

Chapter Eight

Al kept both hands on the steering wheel, classic ten and two, while Fergie kept her hands visible on her lap.

As soon as the two officers got up to the driver's-side and passenger-side windows, they flashed the beams of their lights right where Al had expected them, lighting up their hands first then sweeping toward the glove box, the console, and the floor.

A Port Dexter cop with a face like several miles of bad road had the frowning squint of someone with bitter indigestion—not in love with his job on the night shift. And he was the one with sergeant's stripes. He'd undone the leather strap holding his sidearm in its holster, ready for anything.

He held out a hand without saying anything. Al fished his fake ID out of his wallet and reached ever so slowly to open the glove box and take out the rental agreement, made out with a name that matched. Al caught just a glimpse of the cop on Fergie's side. His flashlight beam was twitching, and he seemed to stand first on one foot and then the other. He, too, was a little overprepared.

But Al most noted Fergie. Her head was lowered so that the bill of her ball cap covered most of her face.

Standard procedure would be for the sergeant, with Smith-Williams on his brass nameplate, to take Al's license back to the still-flashing cruiser to see if he had any outstanding warrants. But he waved the other cop around the rental to take the license and make the short hike.

Al knew the ID would stand up as genuine, so that wasn't a worry. He had a handful in his bag of tricks that would all stand up. The one

Fergie was carrying would be fine as well. He'd gotten them from a reprobate known as Jimmy the Quince, a first-rate forger who claimed to have gone straight—if Al didn't count making the occasional bogus documents for an ex-cop like Al. Jimmy Q not only made passable cards but also uploaded backstory content to help his IDs hold up to close scrutiny. Al wouldn't be likely to get any more such high-quality items from him, since the feds had swooped in a short while later over some bearer bonds Jimmy Q claimed he'd forgotten he'd made.

The sergeant bent closer again and looked hard at Fergie, who was doing her best to share as little of her face as possible.

The cop frowned and straightened again, shaking his head. Al glanced at but tried not to stare at scar tissue on the middle joints of the man's fingers.

When his partner came back and handed the license back to him, the sergeant asked, "What are you doing here?" His tone was pushy, with no need to be civil.

"We'd been over to the bunny bar and wanted a bite to eat. Someone told us about Floy's Place. We just came from there."

"What'd you have?"

"Can you believe he wouldn't serve tomato soup without throwing in a grilled-cheese sandwich?" Al shook his head.

The sergeant relaxed enough that a flicker of a lift showed at the corner of his mouth. "That'd be Floy, all right. Where are you off to now?"

"We're going back to the main strip again, maybe try the Bent Fox's Tail."

The sergeant glanced over at the darkened warehouse. He couldn't have known that Al and Fergie had gotten a quick peek inside. "Well, you'd better just hustle back over that way, then. Get a move on." He handed back Al's fake license and the rental agreement.

Then he leaned closer to frown across at Fergie again and was shaking his head as he stood upright.

Al started the car and was pulling away as the cops were still heading back to their cruiser.

Fergie let out a long breath in a rush.

"You knew that guy, didn't you?" Al glanced at her.

"Yeah. I put him away many moons ago. His name's Lloyd Furbister. And you can damn well bet no one did a background check on that goon unless that's just the sort of person they were after."

"Did he have tattoos?"

"Yeah, on his neck and fingers. The finger tattoos said 'kill' on one hand and 'cops' on the other. He must have had them removed by laser, as much as he could. That wouldn't have been a very good message, given his current employment."

"What did he get sent up for?"

"He was working the old badger game in Austin until half a dozen of the compromised married men he was blackmailing got their heads together and turned on him. It cost some of them their marriages, but they said it was worth it to be shed of a leech like Lloyd. We think he also rolled some of the marks and perhaps even killed one or two, but we had bupkis in the way of hard evidence on that. I didn't think he would be out yet, but I'd lay you even money that there's a parole officer somewhere scratching his head over where this jasper is. I don't know who the other guy was, but he'd had a facial tattoo removed, too, what was probably a tear falling from the corner of his right eye. You know what that means."

"That he was proud of having killed someone. I'm surprised you caught that much, with your head tucked so low."

"I don't mind telling you I was sweating steel-jacketed bullets that they'd tumble to me." She shook her head. "What now?"

"I think we've pushed our luck as far as we should. I'd like to take a closer look at those shrimp boats. They're in the mix somehow, I'm guessing."

"And what a mix it is. We've moved on from a hodgepodge that includes a sniper, helicopter ops, a probable chop shop, and cops who are ex-cons, to guys being moved from bars to motels with factory precision, all in a town that seems to not only frown on but outright discourage family tourism."

"What's all that spell to you?"

"Someone has a helluva cash cow of a revenue stream for as long as they can keep it up without serious prying."

"If bribes are paid, and the city and county cops are on the payroll, how long do you think they could keep up like this?"

"At least a year or more before someone at the state or federal got a whiff of the stink."

"A song by Bobby Ray Champion that got any traction at all would sure have had them sniffing this way."

"That's the shame about Bobby Ray. He was maybe just on the verge of doing something good and a little noble, yet his intentions were just as self-centered and all about personal profit as whoever is running all this."

Al stayed well within the speed limits and kept an eye out for squad cars. He didn't begin to breathe easier until they were leaving Port Dexter, on their way back toward Port Aransas.

As soon as they were quite a way beyond the aura of lights that marked Port Dexter with wavy white lines spreading out into the gulf, Al turned toward the shore, driving past some pretty rough-and-tumble fishing camps that looked abandoned. At last, he could pull off the road and park in a tangle of mesquite, hackberry, and persimmon trees before the shoreline turned to low plants and dunes.

He kept the dome light off and opened the trunk to get his duffel bag. He handed one pair of binoculars to Fergie and kept another for himself.

Fergie was already looking all around. Most of the area was rough and deserted. Only the lights of a cabin two or three hundred yards away showed nearby.

Al handed her one of the small penlights with a cone end so they could keep from tripping over rocks, twigs, or snakes without giving themselves away. He could feel the ground get sandier in spots and could see dried sprays of salt lingering on the leaves of low scrub bushes.

They waded through several stands of tall grasses, following the line of rising ground until they crested a hill and could look out across the gulf toward Port Dexter.

To Al's far right, out on the bouncing chop of waves, a shrimp boat was heading in toward the port. When he swung the glasses back toward the town, he could see two more shrimp boats heading out. It wasn't the right time of day for shrimp boats to be coming in or going out.

Even stranger, one of the outgoing shrimp boats paused near the incoming one while the other outgoing shrimp boat kept going. Twenty minutes later, the boat that had been coming in turned and went out again, while the outgoing boat it had met turned and started back toward the shore.

Al felt a vibration first then heard the sound, a steady *chop, chop, chop* of a machine slicing the air.

He lowered his binoculars. Twin lights in the air were coming toward them. The beams were sweeping back and forth along the shore and far enough above it that they would soon be lighting up Al and Fergie.

One beam shot ahead suddenly and swept across them.

"Get down!" He reached to push her.

But she'd already dived to the ground and tucked as much as possible of herself under the bending branches of a bush. Her hat had fallen off, and her red hair spilled out around her face.

He rolled away from her until he was pressed against the somewhat thorny trunk of a tree.

The copter got to them and paused. The lights darted back and forth where they'd been standing.

Having been on a few nighttime patrols in helicopters, Al could imagine how the scene looked from above. Someone up there must have caught the briefly reflected light from two pairs of binoculars before they'd had a chance to lower them.

Al wished the damned thing would fly on, but it stayed, hovering above them.

Then it lowered, moving closer to the flatter shoreline. A ladder unrolled toward the ground, and two dark figures with what looked like assault rifles strapped to their backs climbed quickly down the ladder.

Al and Fergie got to their feet. She started to turn in the direction of the car, but he touched her arm then pointed in the other direction. The ground there was covered in stone, so going that way, they wouldn't leave tracks.

As soon as the roar of the helicopter lifted, and it began to shine its sweeping lights again, Al could hear the thumping of boots and rustling of men rushing through vegetation toward where he and Fergie had been.

Al was running flat out while trying to stay on the stone and not put a foot down in sand that would leave a print. He glanced back and saw that the two men had split up, and the beam of one light flicking left and right was behind them. The light would be mounted on the assault rifle, probably something even zippier than an AR-15, say something like a Heckler & Koch. Thinking about it didn't help Al move faster.

Fergie's long legs were helping her surge ahead. He grabbed her arm, slowing her, and pointed toward some dry twigs and leaf litter clustered by the wind into a small pile on the stone. She stopped with him and bent close, and he dug out the book of matches he'd gotten at

Bayou Bunny. Fergie moved to block the sea breeze long enough for Al to strike a match. The first one went out in a puff. He bent even closer and tried again. That one caught on some woolly, dry tufts of grass, and a fire smoldered then burst into a small flame. The dried sticks and leaves above soon caught as well.

He tugged at Fergie's arm, and they took off abruptly to the left, where they could loop back, out, and around their pursuer.

The copter moved closer to shine its lights where the fire had become a tiny yellow light. The noise of the copter drowned out any sound their running steps made. They were soon a quarter of a mile away, then a mile away and closer to the highway. An overpass allowed a trickle of a stream to go beneath the road. They slipped inside and moved to the extreme back inside edge, crouching in the darkest shadows. Al put his arms around Fergie's shoulders and was pleased to find she wasn't shaking, just breathing hard.

They stayed there, not moving at all for what seemed several lifetimes but couldn't have been more than an hour.

Finally, the copter lowered in the distance, probably picking up the men, and eventually took off again after a few more sweeps back and forth along the shoreline.

They waited at least another half hour, crouched like a couple of muskrats, listening to traffic pass overhead, before they finally stirred and started the long hike back to where they'd left the rental car.

Even when they got to it, they hesitated, taking a wide and careful loop all the way around it to make sure they weren't walking into a trap.

At last, they slipped inside, and Al fired up the motor and eased out.

When they were back in the flow of traffic at last and just another anonymous car in the night, moving away from Port Dexter, Fergie said, "I don't know about you, but I've had all of that kind of fun I want for one night."

Chapter Nine

The sun was shining so brightly that Fergie flinched as she closed the door to the motel room behind her.

A second-floor Latina maid was standing beside a cleaning cart just a couple of doors away. She glanced toward the Do Not Disturb sign still swaying slightly behind Fergie.

Fergie made the motion of scrubbing under her arms and pointed to the door. Al was still taking his turn in the shower.

The maid gave a patient shrug and went back into the room she was cleaning.

Fergie could see Bonnie below, holding Tanner's leash with Maury standing close. Patty Belle had Little Al in a chest papoose. They all stood near the end of the pool, talking with a woman who looked to be in her fifties or sixties.

She waved back to Bonnie but stayed on the upper level and took out a pad and pen as well as the rumpled matchbook Al had gotten at Bayou Bunny. Her method would be a little old school, but the bar's hat tip to the blast from the past deserved as much.

The tiny print on the side that read Close Cover before Striking said Cumberland Products. She punched in the 800 number on her cell phone.

"How can I help you?"

"I'd like to reorder matchbooks for Bayou Bunny."

"Just a moment. Ah. The same amount, and for all three places?"

"Yes," Fergie said. "And can I confirm the address?"

The sales clerk began to rattle off the addresses of the bars.

"No. I want to make sure the billing address is correct."

"I'm not sure I can give that information out."

"Really? To a customer? Okay. Cancel the order, and I'm switching suppliers."

"Oh. Oh. Just a sec." That time, the clerk gave a different address, which Fergie wrote down.

"Thanks. That's correct." Fergie hung up.

The thread was tiny, but she intended to pull on it.

She went down the stairs and strolled over to the little group.

"This is Mary Doughrety," Bonnie said. "She owns the place."

"So you told me." Fergie turned toward the older woman.

Her dyed-blond hair said she went often to a stylist but hadn't been there that day. The wind lifted and tugged at a curly strand. Mary smiled, but her watery blue eyes didn't join in all the way.

"You certainly have a well-run motel." Fergie glanced about. "Bristol clean, and you keep a close attention on every detail. The place reminds me of a Hilton."

Mary's smile warmed. "Oh, come on, now." But she beamed.

"Bonnie told me you were given an excellent deal on this motel, practically had it handed to you."

"It wasn't exactly free," Mary said. "I don't like to talk about that—can't really."

"But you grew up in Port Dexter, had lived there all your life."

"True. True."

"Yet here you are. Why sell and leave your hometown?"

Mary shifted her weight from one foot to the other, looking around. "I didn't want to sell, but they made me quite an offer," she said. "That's not what did it, though."

"What did?"

"Red did. Red Petersmith. He owned another of the motels there, and he'd always said he'd never sell. Then he did sell and disappeared at the same time. You see, that's the thing. When people start to disappear, then you'd better disappear yourself. So here I am, disappeared the hell away from there."

Al came down the stairs, and Maury started in that direction.

"You'd best make sure your friends get a proper lunch, since they slept right through breakfast time," Mary told Bonnie. "Especially the tall, slim one."

"You're right," Bonnie said. "Fergie's so skinny she thinks cottage cheese is a comfort food. You know what they say. You can lead someone to a chicken fried steak with taters and gravy, but you can't get them to eat it. That's my role on the team." Bonnie patted her little round belly.

"I'm lucky she's there to throw herself on the hand grenade of any large quantities of deep-fried food," Fergie said.

Bonnie patted Mary on the shoulder and led Tanner toward where Maury was meeting Al at the bottom of the stairs.

A tiny frown came and went on Mary's face. But she shook herself and turned to go talk to the maid doing the downstairs rooms. Fergie headed to where the others were moving toward the collection of poolside furniture.

When Al had them all gathered at a round metal table by the pool and mostly in the shade of a beige cantilever umbrella, he said, "What I'm going to suggest has an element of danger. But so does going home and hoping none of Bobby Ray's nosing around comes back to bite us in the butt as I'm convinced it very well can and will."

"I'm in," Maury said.

"You'd better wait until you hear what Al has in mind," Fergie said. "He and I may have worn out our chances to openly nose around over there for now."

"And if you're still as eager after what we tell you, I'm going to ask that you be extra careful. We have found these people, so far, to be extremely vigilant... and damned dangerous."

"DO YOU THINK THAT COPTER was after Al and Fergie specifically, or was it just doing a routine patrol and caught a glimpse of something?" Bonnie asked.

She and Maury were together in their motel room while Patty Belle was changing the baby in the bathroom. Tanner was curled up by the door.

"I don't know what to think for sure, but if I had to guess, I'd say routine. This is an edgy and vigilant town we're looking at. Every effort seems to be taken to keep this their little secret."

"I'm surprised they haven't just killed us. Let's hope they don't rethink that decision."

"Maybe they figured we couldn't know anything at that point." Maury spoke softly, even though waking the baby wasn't a concern. "But figuring out what's going on in this town may be the only thing that saves us."

"Al was vague, keeping his mind open, but what do you think is going on?"

"It's about money, somehow." Maury looked up into her troubled eyes.

"Well, I figured that much."

"And it's enough money to practically hire an army."

"What one thing would do that?"

"I doubt it is one thing. It's probably several carefully orchestrated things, the kind of stuff that has to draw in people, men mainly, and also can be folded up if the heat ever does get an inkling. I would bet they have six months to a year to do all they can then close shop and open up elsewhere."

"What kind of several things are you talking about?"

"You've got boats coming in and going out at odd times. You've got a city police force composed of what may be hardened criminals. I'm sure the sheriff's department has been bought, compromised, or taken over too. You've got black-op helicopters and snipers and who knows what else in the mix."

"That's a lot of effort and money being spent," Bonnie said.

"A whole lot more is probably coming in, and it's more than just a bevy of very young hookers and a possible chop shop."

"On that hooker note..." Bonnie's face stretched tight around a smile she was struggling to achieve. "While you're nosing around in there, trying to find out stuff, you'll leave those young girls alone... won't you?"

"You know you're all I need."

"I'd better be." Her voice was thin and a little high.

She turned toward Patty Belle, who was just coming out of the bathroom with Little Al. Bonnie's fingers flurried through a message to the girl, the gist of which made Patty Belle giggle silently with a hand over her mouth. She put on the papoose and tucked the baby into it, his head leaning against her right away. He looked almost half as big as she was, but she was of sturdy stock and never seemed to mind. She put Tanner's leash on him and headed out the door.

Bonnie locked the door and turned to Maury.

"What do you think? The baby and the dog are off for a stroll around the pool, a Do Not Disturb sign is on the door, and we're alone together while Al and Fergie return the rental and get something else. What do you say to something extra special?"

"You don't have to ask me twice." Maury had his shirt half off and was trying to unbuckle his belt at the same time. "Extra special. Zow!"

Chapter Ten

Maury got out of the back seat of a Jeep Cherokee. Al had managed to rent it for a day from a mechanic's shop that kept spare cars for patrons while their vehicles were being serviced. Mary Doughrety claimed that the mechanic's keeping her 1999 Ford Ranger running was allowing her to maintain a profit margin with the motel. That may have been a stretch, but Al said they needed something different, and they'd turned in the Enterprise rental car as soon as they had something else.

Maury watched Al and Fergie pull away and felt the yank of his last lifeline tugging away from him. He was on his own.

No use looking back. He turned and headed toward the green front door beneath the pink and orange neon lights that spelled out Bayou Bunny. A little set of rabbit ears acted as an exclamation point, as though the place was going to be some kind of Playboy Club. *Look out, Hugh Hefner. Here I come.*

He swung the door open and went inside, nearly coughing in the layer of hazy smoke. Maury had been in a lot of clubs in his day, back when he was something of a horndog—a character trait Bonnie had worked on, in part with a small cast-iron skillet, the rest by being younger and wearing him out in bed.

An empty table in the dim lights of the far corner called to him. He could watch and have his back to the wall. Only half the tables were populated, but a hum of constant conversation and clinking of glasses filled the air. A subdued version of U2 singing that they still hadn't found what they were looking for came from hidden speakers.

He had barely slid into the seat when a petite young girl with large black eyes, black hair in a short page boy cut, and skin the color of pecan pie came to stand beside him.

"Do you want company?"

"Sure," Maury said.

She eased into the seat beside him. "My name's Marza. Are you the bottle-of-champagne sort of fella or the tall-cold-long-neck-beer sort?"

"I'm the Diet Coke–and–rum sort. But I'm really not much of a drinker."

A waitress, slightly older and a little surly looking, was heading their way.

"Oh? What is it you like to do?"

"We could skip the drinking if you know someplace."

"Oh, I know someplace. We'll go right now, but you'd better leave a tip, a nice one, or Janey there is apt to get unhappy."

Maury took out a ten and put it on the table. Janey stared down at it but didn't reach for it. Maury waited.

Janey's frown intensified.

"Nicer than that," Marza said. "No drinks just now, Janey."

Maury added another ten. It wasn't for service. It was for nothing. But Janey scooped it up as her due and spun and was off through the haze.

Marza took Maury's hand and tugged him toward the hallway, where a sign read Restrooms.

They went right past those. She swung open the door to the outside and led him through. The night air seemed cool and fresh, with the salty tang of a coastal town. They had to take only a few steps across a parking lot.

Inside the motel office, a sign beside the check-in desk gave the rates, which started at one hundred bucks an hour.

The man behind the counter was shorter than Maury, had thinning gray hair and big ears, wore black-rimmed glasses, and used red suspenders over a white shirt. "You gonna be longer than an hour?"

"I can't imagine why." Maury handed over a hundred-dollar bill from the thousand dollars Al had given him from his duffel bag while saying he sure hoped that would be enough.

The room was on the ground floor and looked like every motel room Maury had ever been inside. A low beige unit beneath the heavily draped windows provided a low hum of air conditioning.

A framed faux painting on the wall showed the same cheap print of an ocean shoreline of waves he'd seen in half a dozen other places. Most of the furniture was bolted into place.

As soon as they were inside, Marza reached up and started to unbutton her pink blouse. "It's gonna be three hundred unless you want something fancy... or kinky."

"I just want to talk." He saw the startled look in her widening eyes. "But I'll pay."

He put the money on the oak veneer surface of the combination desk and chest of drawers.

"Okay." She kept taking her clothes off. "You mind if I grab a quick shower first? I didn't get a chance after the last... gentleman."

Her body had the same soft brown hue as that pecan-pie face. The skin was taut, her breasts pert, and she put a little wiggle into her rear as she scampered into the bathroom.

With the sound of the shower going like a tiny indoor waterfall, Maury looked around the room and tried to put his mind on what niggled at him, what seemed just a little eerie and threatening. The place wasn't entirely different from where they'd rescued Patty Belle. But something was putting him far more on edge. While watching those nature videos where the bee messed about on the lip of a carnivorous pitcher plant, about to fall in, he wanted to yell, "Watch out!" That was the sort of warning tickle he felt coursing through him at the moment.

She didn't take long and soon came out wrapped in a white towel, rubbing at the ends of her hair, which she'd gotten wet without meaning to.

"Did you come by yourself?" she asked.

"Yeah."

"Are you a single fella with no one waiting at home?"

Maury sensed those were the stock questions and were fraught with danger if he answered wrongly. "I have a wife," he said, "and a small child. I just wanted to get away and talk to someone else, anyone. But I'm fortunate to come across someone as attractive as you. Were you born in America?"

Her pretty forehead wrinkled. "Are you sure about being with me, not playing? I'm all wet, clean, and shiny." She opened her towel to give him a quick flash of a look at her.

He swallowed. "No. Let's just talk."

"You don't find me attractive?"

"Oh my, yes."

"You're not weird or something, are you?"

"The jury's still out on that."

"You really have a wife and child waiting?"

He sensed that was part of the script and did something he'd been told not to do. Al had told him to leave his wallet with Bonnie, but Maury had taken a photo out of it first, a laminated shot of Bonnie holding Little Al. He slid it out of his pocket and held it out.

She looked at it closely then at him. "She's so... much younger than you."

"What can I say? I can be a smooth talker, and I'm a very lucky man."

Marza handed the photo back and started to reach for her clothes. "Are you sure?"

"Yeah, let's just talk."

"It's your money."

It's Al's money.

"Why pay for something you don't get?"

"Do you enjoy doing this?"

"Twenty times a day? What do you think? Some of us take pain killers or drink. I don't. But it's not a day at the beach, like we'd get to go and do that."

He shook his head.

"You haven't forgotten how, have you?" she asked him. "How to do it?"

"Oh, I know. I used to be quite the willing fellow that way. But I've gotten a taste of something new. I love my wife and have learned respect. Now, I'm about family. Family is everything."

She'd tugged on her jeans and was reaching for her pink blouse. She stopped and looked at him then started to say something, but the words caught in her throat.

He knew he'd touched a nerve. "Do you ever feel anything for your... clients?"

"What do you mean?"

"Do you kiss them?"

"Do you want to be kissed?"

"No. I was just wondering."

"We can and are encouraged to do so. After all, it's the least we can do, considering, for some of them."

"What?"

"Oh, I can't say."

"You weren't born into a happy family in America?" he tried again.

"No. El Salvador." Her eyes widened for a second. "But I have papers. We're not supposed to... Let's talk about you."

She pulled on the blouse and began to button it.

"Naw. I'm hardly interesting at all. But you are. How did you come to be here?"

She hesitated then frowned. "It was love. Love got me here." She spat out the word *love* like it was the worst of four-letter words and finished buttoning the blouse with a little vehemence.

"How so?"

"I was thirteen, and we lived in what I've come to hear called a shanty town in San Salvador, in a home we'd made ourselves out of what could be found. Every time there was a hard rain, we had to almost start over. One wall was corrugated iron, the others bits of wood and cardboard. We had no plumbing, none at all. There were six of us kids with no dad. He was gone before I really knew him. Then Felipe came along. He loved me... he said. Plus, it was a way to get out of there, away from the way I lived."

Maury nodded, encouraging her.

"But when we ran away, there was another boy there too. He helped us get across, into America, into a place called Houston. I thought I was going to be married to Felipe, but I found he had sold me. Then I had to work, doing... you know."

She was slipping on her shoes and looked up at him. Her face was a mixture of bitter sadness and a dare for him to say anything bad about her.

Maury looked at her. *There's a little girl in there—inside her. One who never got a chance to grow up as or even act as, play, or be a little girl as long as she should have.*

"You poor thing," Maury wanted to reach out and give her a comforting hug, but he knew better. "What you've been through..."

Her face flushed a darker hue. "Oh, I shouldn't have said any of that. You've got to just forget I said anything at all."

"That was a long time ago?"

"At least four years. But enough of that."

Maury was doing the math in his head. She'd said she was thirteen when she took off with Felipe. That made her seventeen at the moment.

She glanced toward the door. "I don't know what made me... I was just having a bad day, and you seemed... nice. Please don't tell anyone that I said anything."

"Don't worry. I knew someone like you a very long time ago, a little older but full of pep and vim and a joy for life. I thought I was in love with her. Maybe I was. But I didn't do anything about it. I was too busy in those days, making idle conquests. Love. What did I know about it?"

"Well, I will tell you one thing." Marza's words held an edge that grew in intensity. "I will *never* fall in love again. *Ever!*"

Maury had enough of a hazy picture that he thought he should call Al and have him pick him up. Maybe he and Fergie had added more to the perspective from their end and would have enough to at least call in for outside help.

A knock on the door was followed by "Police. Open up."

A look at Marza's face told Maury she was as surprised as he was. That sort of thing had happened before, but she sure didn't expect it at that moment.

Chapter Eleven

The lights of the city faded behind them. The businesses then the houses also thinned until Al was driving through a small collection of sizeable homes set off from the core of the town, a little higher up, on estate-sized plots of land, and many of them were fenced off. A different sort of people lived in those homes, ones whose children probably didn't attend public schools and certainly didn't take their lunches from home in brown paper bags the way Al had as a boy.

He drove right past the address they'd gotten as the billing office for the bar's matchbook orders, taking in two large granite pillars on either side of a security gate of black metal bars with a crest above it. Stone walls ran in either direction from the gate, old and established enough to be the kind in which he could expect to find shards of broken glass embedded at the top.

"Hmm. Hmm. Hmm." Fergie shook her head.

"That's sure no office building," Al said. "It's some sort of mansion and a damned secure one."

To their left, a greenbelt had been preserved as a buffer, perhaps a park or just woodlands, and ran alongside the road, between the houses and the coastal city below. Al had to drive past three more estate entrances before he found one that might be more accessible. An overgrown lane to the left went into the woods for a few yards and stopped at a fence, but it was far enough away from the road to hide the Cherokee and give them a starting point.

Al turned off the dome light and handed Fergie one of the penlights with a cone on its end to limit its light to a minimum when it was needed.

The moon was nearly full, so they didn't have to turn on their lights right away except when in the shadow of a partial canopy of live oak limbs above the lane.

At the road, they waited until they could hear no sounds of any vehicles coming from either direction. They scurried across, slipped through a gap in a hedge of boxwood bushes, and stayed low in a shadow that ran alongside a green wall.

He took each boot step with care, pleased that he couldn't hear Fergie's steps at all. The wind rustled the treetops and occasionally swirled the leaf litter at their feet.

A dog, a big one, was barking in the distance, but it was either chained in place or behind a fence. The sound wasn't moving toward them.

They had to climb over one waist-high stone wall and skirt around the lights of a nearly mansion-sized home before coming to the address they were after.

Al held up a hand.

The only break in the solid stone that rose ten feet above the ground was a thick-barred metal gate that looked rusted shut. Nevertheless, someone had added some seriously thick chains and a couple of padlocks to seal it even further.

Al eased close to the gate and shined his light through the bars.

"Yep."

"Yep what?"

"Even from here, I can see trip wires. I bet they're backed by laser beams for the unfortunate trespasser who tries to step over the trip wires."

"No spraying an aerosol can at them to find them, is there?"

"You know that's so much television hooey. If they're any good, you'd probably set them off with a spray. But this place is security crazy."

He could see the main buildings, a big house and a four-car garage. By day, it probably looked like the other moneyed estates in that little elite part of Port Dexter—in stark contrast to the town itself and the shoreline businesses.

"Probably more booby traps scattered throughout the wooded area," Fergie whispered, "and then there's that wide-open area around the main buildings."

A strong breeze moved the low shrubs around the main building enough to make motion-sensor spotlights flicker on and off. Cameras probably covered every angle as well.

A man wearing a black vest and holding an automatic weapon came out of a door at the end of the garage and started around the house, looking around as he went.

"I think we can write off any more nosing around than this for the night. But at least we learned something." Al turned to start back toward where they'd left the Cherokee.

"I'm surprised we haven't heard from Maury. I expected him to want to be taken back to Bonnie and the baby by now. You don't think he's fooling around, do you?"

"I think he knows better," Al said. "And what's more, he changed. He could say no and mean it now."

"I sure hope you're right."

WHEN MARZA OPENED THE door, the two uniformed cops came bustling in and went right for Maury.

"I didn't send anything," Marza said. "No text messages."

Ignoring her, they spun Maury around, tugged his arms behind his back, and slapped handcuffs on his wrists. She started toward them, and a sergeant with Smith-Williams on his nametag lifted an arm to backhand her. Marza retreated with quick steps.

While not entirely ignoring the stockier and shorter cop, Maury stayed focused on the sergeant, Smith-Williams, whom Fergie had told him was an ex-con named Lloyd Furbister. Even if she hadn't said any-thing, Maury might have picked up on the hardness of the eyes that prison time could give a man.

"I didn't say anything about him yet," she said.

"You didn't need to."

Maury knew the men weren't ones to kid around with, and they certainly weren't real everyday cops but something far worse. His insides went limp, and he let them manhandle him for the time being, hoping he could bide his time and figure out what the hell was going on.

AS THEY DROVE BACK into town, Fergie peered down every street they passed. She didn't really expect to see Maury, but that was better than doing nothing. She was trying hard not to think about what might've gone wrong. Maybe he'd just forgotten or gotten busy. Things would be best for him if he hadn't gotten busy in the wrong way and Bonnie found out.

Fergie's phone vibrated in her pocket. She'd forgotten she had switched it over when they were creeping about outside. She answered it.

"Have you heard from Maury?"

"No, Bonnie. Did you?"

"Nope. Something's up. He said he would call."

"We're on our way to go check on him. He's supposed to be done and should be waiting for us."

"Then why didn't he call?" Bonnie asked.

"That's what we intend to find out." Fergie hung up as Al pulled up across the street from Bayou Bunny.

Al was looking across the street.

"Uh-oh. The other direction," Fergie said.

She was watching two policemen lead Maury out of the motel and toward their cruiser. Maury's wrists were handcuffed behind his back. One cop pressed down on Maury's head as he shoved him into the back seat while the other went around and got into the driver's side.

"Nope. Not good at all," Al said.

THE TWO COPS HOLDING Maury's upper arms as they led him into the police station were pinching him far harder than was necessary. At his age, he bruised easily and could practically feel black-and-blue handprints forming. They didn't care, and he suspected that he wouldn't either, for long, if things went the way they seemed to be headed.

The desk sergeant who looked up at them as they entered had the same hard eyes and was another ex-con, probably. *Want to feel helpless?* Maury thought. *Try seeking help in a town where the cops are the worst people you might meet.*

They made him empty his pockets into a manila envelope. He missed the cell phone most of all as it went in.

"No car keys?"

"I got a ride into town from a stranger."

He noticed they didn't even go to the bother of writing the name from the fake ID onto it. They patted him down and took his belt and shoestrings. He'd heard that was to keep despondent prisoners from hanging themselves. He felt pretty down but not enough for that. He would never go that route. The picture of Bonnie and Little Al in his head would keep him fighting to stay alive.

The two cops dragged him to a more dimly lit back hallway that ran along a row of cells with heavy metal bars. The air smelled of dust, dried sweat, and stale urine. They tugged him along until they got to the last cell then took off his handcuffs. One of them opened the door, and the other swung Maury inside. As they turned away, they pulled out their wooden nightsticks and sent them clattering down the hall to slam into the far wall.

They were laughing hysterically as they headed back up the hallway. The metal door clanged shut with a note of finality Maury didn't care for at all.

Rubbing his arms, he looked down at a hunched figure sitting on a steel cot hung in place with thick chains. Only a single bulb in a cage high overhead lit up the cell, and Maury suspect it was only a forty-watt light.

The man on the cot lifted his head and looked at Maury. He was quite a bit younger, maybe late thirties or early forties. He'd been crying. His eyes were bloodshot, and his cheeks flushed red. "I should never have told her a thing."

"Who?" Maury asked.

"The girl, a tight little Asian unit, said she used to live in Bangkok. She kept asking me, 'You come here alone?' and 'Did you tell no one you here?' That's when the gong should have gone off. Now they have my SUV too. I only bought it six weeks ago. I watched them hook it up and tow it away as I was hauled away myself."

Maury took a moment or two to go over the sort of questions Marza had asked him: "Did you come by yourself?" "Are you a single fella, with no one waiting at home?"

As Maury's eyes adjusted to the dim light in the cell, he reappraised his cellmate as being closer to late twenties. He'd just had a hard time of it in the past few hours, which had aged him or worn him down.

"My name's Edgar, by the way." He held out a hand without standing.

Maury was adding up the bits of information and details he'd gathered so far and combined those with what Al and Fergie had shared. The clearer the picture got, the worse he felt about it.

Young girls, many probably underage, were being brought in from all over. Men in the know were coming to the town to see them. Those the girls discovered were on their own got flagged, like Edgar. Their vehicles probably ended up in that chop shop with the pieces going into the currently hyper-eager parts market.

He still hadn't parsed out what happened to the men, but it couldn't be good.

Then he remembered the shrimp boats that went out and came in at odd times—not out shrimping, that was for sure. He wondered if they brought in the women—girls, really. He'd heard nothing about drugs so far. No one seemed to be trying to buy or sell any. But that didn't mean they weren't a small part of whatever the hell was going on.

The door to the cells opened with a clang, and men were talking and laughing. From the sounds, he gathered men were being taken out of the cells.

When the two men in black got to Maury's cell, one said, "Just got room for one more this trip."

One of them started toward Maury.

"No. Not that one."

They made Edgar stand and put on the handcuffs. They had to hold him upright. He was sobbing, and his legs had gone to rubber. Still, they managed to move him out of the cell and head him down the hallway after clanging Maury's cell door shut.

The last of his questions had been answered. He had the beginning of an idea of what happened to the men. The town was a sticky fly trap for a good number of them.

He didn't know why he'd been spared. He figured there must have been a reason but couldn't think of a good one. So far, everything seemed like it was happening to someone else.

With all the other prisoners gone, the area was quiet except for the sound of pipes thumping and thrumming in the thick stone walls.

He was all by himself and didn't care much for the privacy. All he could think about was his cell phone and how much he wished he could make a couple of calls.

EDGAR'S HANDCUFFS WERE too tight, but he didn't say anything about them. One of the men in the line ahead of him had done so and had gotten backhanded across the side of his head for speaking at all.

In that hushed silence, with just their shoes scuffing along on the sidewalk then asphalt, he had way too much time to think.

"Faster." A cop nudged him from behind with a nightstick. That was the first any of them had spoken, and it was the last.

The line of men was led not to a regular police vehicle but to a dark windowless van. Within, the cop nearest Edgar used a plastic cable tie to fasten his handcuffs to a rail behind him. That made the ride uncomfortable after the van's doors closed because he was jerked around when it took off, but his personal comfort meant very little at the moment.

When the van finally came to a stop, the back doors were opened, and the cops stood on either side as the men were led away one by one by two men in black combat gear with AR-15s over their shoulders and wearing combat masks of silver and black skulls. Since he'd been last in, Edgar was first out. One of the men in black used a KA-BAR knife to cut the tie holding Edgar to the rail and yanked him out to stumble along as they both held an arm and led him up a gangway onto the deck of a shrimp boat. Once there, they led him down a hallway to a room that looked empty except for steel rings fastened to the wooden floor. They pushed him down, undid his cuffs, slipped one end through the ring, and fastened them again. He knew speaking was useless, and they stood and went to get the others.

Once they were all inside and fastened to the floor, the door slammed shut on them. Someone was crying, big sobs coming nonstop. Another was trying to throw up but was only getting dry heaves. The smell of their collective fear filled the room, almost overcoming the stink of diesel fumes.

The boat lurched and soon took on the motion of climbing waves as it headed out into the gulf. The men in the room were reduced to rough sounds, no words, except one guy who wanted his mother but was shushed by the others.

All too soon, the boat stopped and swayed in the waves. The door opened, and the armed men freed one of the men and took him out the door. One by one, they all were taken away. Again, since he had been first into the room, he was the last out.

Out on the swaying deck, he looked about at the sea at dusk, at the raised nets of the shrimp boat, and toward the helm, where the captain and what looked like a first mate were looking ahead, keeping the boat as steady as they could in the swell of waves as they kept the boat moving steadily along. Neither looked his way as he was led to the lee-side gunwale.

He expected one of the men to say something as they removed his cuffs. Instead, he got a hearty shove from behind and went sailing over the side to splash into water that was surprisingly cold.

The boat kept moving, and the two armed men moved across the deck and out of sight.

He knew not to yell but did instinctively start swimming back toward the boat. But it picked up speed, fading from view. It must have been heading back toward shore, he figured, so he swam that way, following it until his arms tired and he had to gasp for air. The boat moved farther and farther away, getting smaller, until it was out of sight. The chill was going through him. No sharks were swimming around him, but his arms and legs were turning into lead and shivering at the same time.

The boat was out of sight, and none of the other men were nearby in the water as he'd expected. He thought for a second or two about people falling asleep in the snow and not waking. He tried to keep moving his arms and kicking his legs, but they were too heavy. Edgar felt exhausted, and his eyes were closing as he slipped beneath the next rising wave.

Chapter Twelve

Al waited until the police cruiser had gone half a block then eased into the sparse traffic and followed not too closely. He could see Maury's head through the back window.

When the car pulled up in front of the police station, an older, sprawling yellow brick building, Al drove past and came around the block again to park far enough away that they wouldn't arouse suspicion.

"Are you thinking of rushing them before they get Maury inside?" Fergie asked.

"Not these guys."

From that distance, they watched Maury, still in handcuffs, get led into the building.

"There isn't anything about this that feels good," Fergie said, "especially when I know that sergeant is Furbister."

"I'm betting the whole department is made up of Furbister's sort," Al said. "If the sheriff's department is also infiltrated by ex-cons, we'll have to be extra careful."

Fergie's hands tightened into fists on her lap. "I feel so helpless. If this were any other town, we could talk to the cops and do what we could to free Maury."

"I'll be surprised if they plan to hold him in a cell for long. All we can do now is wait and watch."

"I wish we could just call some of your federal friends."

"We still don't have enough of anything solid to call for outside help. Besides, most of my so-called fed friends are people who put up with me rather than became friends, except maybe Jaime Avila, and he's

ICE, which probably doesn't apply here." Al was squeezing the steering wheel tightly and made himself stop. "I wish I knew what Maury knows by now. It must be something, maybe enough. Then we could make that call."

After an hour, several prisoners were brought out and loaded into a black van. None of them was Maury.

When the van came back half an hour later, two men in black combat gear, complete with masks, went inside and led Maury out to the van. While Furbister and the other cop had looked formidable, those guys looked even more so. Though they didn't carry long guns like those closely guarding the estate they'd visited, Al could see what they were packing on their gun belts. *Kind of odd,* he thought, *for guys looking like that to waltz into and back out of a police station unless something is pretty rotten in Denmark.*

"Now?" she asked.

"Not yet."

Maury was the only person in their load. The unmarked vehicle took off as soon as the doors shut—a windowless van slipping off into the night, nobody's dream of a good time.

Fergie said, "I hope nothing really bad happens to Maury because we didn't do something."

"Oh, we're going to do something."

Al turned on the engine and followed.

THE MEN IN BLACK DIDN'T pinch Maury's upper arms as much when they led him out of the van, toward a shrimp boat waiting at a dock. But he didn't read anything like gentleness into their handling of him. They both looked at him with uncaring eyes from behind their masks, which looked like silver-and-black skulls. They barely bothered to glance at him at all, as if he were a slab of dead meat. He imagined they'd had opportunity to get quite callous about what they were doing. Those masks were probably meant to evoke terror, but Maury didn't need them, since he already had a pretty good case of the heebie-jeebies.

Gulls were gathering around the boat, some patently waiting, others dipping and soaring closer, excited about the possibility of fish. Maury regretted for a second, for the birds' sake, that the nets would probably not be dipped on that run.

Over the smell of the diesel engine, running and warm after having already made a run out into the gulf and back, Maury could smell the aroma of dried shrimp and probably squid as they led him across the weathered deck. He wondered if the boat and its crew even bothered to go shrimping as often as before, having found an even more lucrative source of revenue.

As the smell grew richer—and riper—he figured they did a bit of both. He wasn't too keen, though, on the thought that he might well be chum before the night was done.

The two men led him to a small room that had been converted into what looked like a sturdy brig. Its deck had been freshly hosed, so the wood glowed dark and looked slightly damp around a line of fastened steel rings. The walls looked solid as well.

They undid his cuffs long enough to lower him to the deck, slip one end through a ring, and fasten his wrists again. They stood and, without a glance back at him, went out the door.

Maury was the only passenger that time, though he could imagine the room crowded with all the men who'd made the earlier trip. None of what he was picturing made him feel better.

He expected the boat to start up and take off, but it seemed to be waiting.

He finally heard someone fiddling as they unlocked the door. When it swung open, Al and Fergie came bustling in. They were on their own, coming to his rescue.

"Al," Maury said, too late.

The two men in black combat gear, both wearing their masks of silver and black skulls, rushed in behind them with AR-15s pointed at Al's and Fergie's backs.

"I wanted to tell you guys that they were using me as bait."

Maury could tell from Al's face, and that he was slower to lower his gun to the deck, that he was calculating his chances of turning and firing.

The boat began to move while the men were still lowering Al and Fergie to the hard boards and slipping handcuffs through the rings to hold them in place.

The men in black took their cell phones and pistols and Al's wallet. They left the makeshift brig and closed the door with a firm, assertive click.

Maury looked from Al's face to Fergie's. "Sorry, guys. I wish I could have warned you."

"They seem to know a lot more about us than they should," Al said.

"Mary Doughrety?" Fergie asked.

"It's possible. Make that probable. They didn't just give her a new motel and her life. They probably own a bit of her now."

"I wish she could have just told us who's behind all this," Maury said.

"That's not how that sort of thing works, Maury," Fergie replied.

"I can't say that I really want to know how it works, only how to make it unwork."

The shrimp boat bounced as it left the dock and climbed the swells. Each time they rose, they came back down onto the wood, but that was the least of their worries. They were being taken out into the gulf.

BONNIE TUCKED LITTLE Al into the crib, and she and Patty Belle stood watching him for a few moments. He had the gift Bonnie wished she possessed. His eyes closed, and he almost immediately conked out.

She was sleepy herself but knew she couldn't sleep until she heard from Maury.

Tanner curled up on the floor beside the crib.

"Even you are better at relaxing than me," she told the dog.

Patty Belle went over to her rollaway bed, sat down, and took out a super-soft brush from the backpack holding all her possessions. She brushed at her wispy pale-blond hair the way she'd seen Bonnie do with her own curly darker-golden locks.

Bonnie was heading toward her own bed to sit down and wait when Tanner sat up, stared at the door, and gave a low growl while his lips curled back from his teeth.

Bonnie rushed to her suitcase, pulled out her .38 Chief's Special, and went to stand beside the door.

A key clicked in the lock.

The door opened, and the barrel of a gun started through. Tanner's growl turned into a roar, and he charged. The gun barrel lowered to point at him.

Bonnie stepped quickly into the doorway and saw two men in black combat gear, bulletproof vests, gun belts, and facemasks that looked like silver-and-black skulls. They were meant to scare before the men killed, but she had a half-second drop on them.

She caught the eyes of the first man in black widening as he tried to lift the gun barrel back up to point at her.

Her arm extended, she squeezed the trigger at almost point-blank range, and a hole appeared where an eye had been. Before he could even fall, she spun to the other one, whose mouth was open in surprise. He tried to step around the falling man, and she shot him once in the head and again in the neck and body as he fell.

The shots woke the baby, who began to cry. Bonnie glanced that way. Patty Belle was already at the crib, having put her own pudgy little body between the baby and the door, protecting him with all she had to give, her own life. Bonnie shook her head. Patty Belle's eyes were faintly pink and moist but bravely fixed on Bonnie. That little girl had seen and experienced a lot in her life, violence most people could only imagine. But as long as Bonnie was beside her to protect her, she would believe she would be okay.

Bonnie stepped over the bodies to peer around and see if more were coming. But apparently, those two were all of them.

She rushed back into the room, put the baby in its papoose, shoved what she could into her suitcase, and clipped on Tanner's leash. Patty Belle had her backpack on, ready to go. They headed out the door, Patty Belle daintily stepping over the two bodies. Neither of them looked back until they were a couple of blocks away and still moving as quickly as their feet could carry them.

Bonnie started to reach for her cell phone to call Maury, but she stopped herself. If he could've called, he would have. She, Patty Belle, her baby, and the dog were on their own for the moment.

Thinking as quickly as she could, she eased over onto the back streets, and they started in the direction of the storage shed where they'd parked Fergie's car. Patty Belle's eyes stayed fixed on Bonnie, who had a notion to leave town as quickly as she could. That area was no safer for them than Port Dexter.

Chapter Thirteen

The boat was rising and dropping as it climbed the swells, going out into the gulf. The stale smell of diesel fumes didn't help fend off Al's twinge of sea sickness, nor did the lingering odor of stale sweat and dried vomit from others who had previously succumbed to being in that small room. Al didn't imagine they would have to go far, if the crew's intention was just to bung them over the side one by one. He based that on how long the shrimp boat had been gone when they'd taken the batch of men before Maury out to sea.

"This is the worst," Fergie said, "having to sit here on the floor and wait, not being able to do anything about it. We're so utterly helpless."

"I don't know about that." Maury lifted one arm. His handcuffs were only on one wrist.

"How did you do that?" Fergie asked.

Maury reached up and undid the other cuff. Then he went over to Al's handcuffed wrists.

"Maury spent all that time learning to be a homespun magician to do parties. I'm betting he had a bobby pin in one sock." Al had a note of admiration in his tone along with affection for his once-estranged brother, who had just come in very handy.

Al rubbed his wrists while Maury freed Fergie.

"Now what?" Fergie asked as she stood.

"Time for one of your ear-splitting, earth-shattering screams," Al said.

"I don't have one of those."

"Then time to improvise."

Maury put his hands over his ears.

Al moved over to stand just inside the door.

Fergie took a deep breath and let out a high-pitched lungful of a scream that Alfred Hitchcock himself would have awarded an Oscar.

Footsteps came running to the door, it was tugged open, and one of the armed masked men started in, leading with his barrel.

Al stepped close, jerked the AR-15 from the man's hands, and smashed the butt of it across the face of the second man heading inside. The first man spun toward Al but forgot or disrespected Fergie, who kicked into the vee of the man's crotch from behind with a punt that would have scored a fifty-yard field goal. He dropped to the deck, clutching himself.

The second man in black put his hands to his face and dropped his weapon as Al yanked him inside and hit him again with the gun butt, that time on the back of his head. He gave the other guy the same treatment, a thump to the head, and they both lay stretched out on the deck. He hadn't been particularly gentle with the two, who he suspected would not have winced when they threw Al and the others overboard.

On a whim, Al yanked the combat masks off. Both hard-faced men had buzz cuts, one so closely clipped he looked almost bald. Al didn't recognize either, but he knew the type—men with a great deal of experience and no conscience or qualms whatsoever, who would sell their services to anyone with enough money. He'd seen mercenaries like that working for the Mexican drug cartels. One such killer from the States had initiated the practice of cutting off heads and hanging them from bridges to send a harsh message, and Al had suspected the man had gotten some secret joy from doing so.

"Handcuff them to the rings and gag them." Al turned the gun around and eased out the door to see if anyone else was coming. "All clear," he said when he went back into the brig to admire their work. "The boat is probably running with a light crew, since they didn't plan on dropping their nets."

Fergie picked up the other AR-15, an eager gleam in her eyes.

Maury lifted two pistols, Fergie's Glock and Al's Sig Sauer. "They had these in their belts. But our cell phones are gone. They must have thrown them overboard, and they don't seem to have any of their own."

"Did you get their keys?" Al asked.

Maury held up two sets then took the tiny handcuff key off one set and put it in his pocket. "For good luck."

They slipped into the hallway. Maury turned to lock the brig's door behind them. No sounds came from inside.

Al held up a finger. Maury moved close behind him. Fergie kept her weapon covering behind them.

As they appeared on the deck, one hand saw them and the weapons they carried. He dropped a net he was mending and without even a smattering of hesitation jumped headfirst over the side.

Al debated for a second then reached for a red-and-white life preserver ring and hurled it overboard—no sense letting a man who didn't look like one of the heavies drown. He had probably stood by while others were pushed overboard, but Al didn't know enough to judge absolutely.

They looked around carefully but saw no one until they got to the helm. The captain inside looked like an older sea salt who'd spent most of his life on the water. He was leaning far back in his chair, with one white rubber boot on the large wooden steering wheel. He watched a screen on his left and kept an eye on the open gulf ahead. He didn't seem to have heard a thing or have any reason for alarm until he spun and stared at Al and Fergie's weapons.

He tried to grab upward for the mic of the ship-to-shore radio while reaching at the same time for a pistol lying beside the computer screen. He should have picked one or the other. Fergie's long legs took her across to him, and with the barrel of her gun, she knocked the gun out of his hand as he lifted it. Then she held the barrel to his face. Al thought his other hand went upward to put the mic back in its holder. Then he caught a glitter in the old salt's eyes, more cantankerous and stubborn than mischievous. He yanked down hard, tearing the connecting wire away and ripping the front of the ship-to-shore radio halfway from its mounting.

Then the captain reached for a lever and pulled it, starting the grind of something large moving.

Fergie yanked the captain out of his chair and sent him sprawling onto the wooden deck.

Al rushed forward. "He's started to raise the lowered outriggers. If they come all the way up, we'll wallow about with all the heavy nets held out in the air the way they are." He had to push the lever hard, but he got the outriggers started down again.

The shrimp boat steadied as the outriggers lowered again, but it was turning in the wave sets and would soon be sideways.

"I hope you know how to pilot a boat like this." Fergie kept her gun pointed at the captain, who hadn't tried to rise. His expression registered fear, shame, and at the same time, amazingly, a smirk of suppressed confidence.

Al went to the wheel and straightened the bow. "How hard can it be? It's only a few thousand times as big as my bass boat."

The truth was that it was far harder than he'd expected.

Going in a straight line and trying to keep the bow pointed into the sides of waves was one thing, but turning a top-heavy boat around with waves coming from various directions was far more difficult. He had to give begrudging admiration to the captain, who had been steering with one foot. It took much of Al's strength to turn the boat, and he was almost jerked out of the seat a couple of times.

After several awkward moments, Al said, "Let's get him back up here."

As Fergie lifted the man off the deck and eased him to the steering spot behind the wheel, she asked, "Are you going to behave?"

He nodded eagerly, but Al noticed the man's glimmer of a smirk again for a moment. He'd known handling a shrimp boat was going to be too much for Al, who reached to his back pocket and took out the handcuffs Maury had removed from his wrists.

"Cuff him to the wheel."

"Not the wheel." The captain's eyes pleaded. "I need to be able to turn her."

"Okay, then." Al turned to Fergie. "See if you can find a stretch of chain. His chair's bolted to the deck."

She came back with a two-foot-long stretch of sturdy-looking new chain.

The captain shrugged as she cuffed his left wrist to the chain once she wrapped it around the base of his chair.

He glanced at the guns they held and fussed with the cuff a bit, but he managed to turn the ship around so that they could start back toward the shore.

They hadn't gone far before Al saw a dot ahead bobbing up and down on the swells.

"There's the guy who went overboard." Fergie pointed to where a sailor clutched the red-and-white life ring.

The captain rose from his chair, as far as his chained left wrist would let him. "Oh my heavenly stars. That's Luke Boy. What's he doing out there?"

"He jumped," Al said.

"I'll pull the old gal up close if you can get him back on board," the captain said.

Al asked Fergie, "Do you think you and Maury can get him on board and below to the brig?"

"Yep. I saw a whole bucket of handcuffs down there."

"Not Luke Boy. He's as harmless as a mouse, and I need him. He's not like those others."

Al looked into the captain's eyes and decided he was shooting straight.

"Okay. Just get him on board, and put a blanket around him," Al said. "He's probably halfway to hypothermia by now."

While she scurried away to get Maury and a blanket, the captain looked up at Al. "I appreciate that. I rightly do. Luke Boy's not smart, but he's a steady hand. I promised his mother I'd look after him. She's someone I... knew for a spell. Boy might even be my son."

Al was looking across the gulf and, for brief flickers, was letting himself just be on the water. Pelicans bobbed near the slowing boat, and gulls dipped low to have a look. A silver edge lined the crests of waves where swells weren't merely lifting and falling. What whiff of wind came into the cabin had a taste of salt to it.

He looked down. Luke Boy was giving them difficulties. He didn't want to come in.

The captain keyed a loudspeaker and shouted into it. "Give it up, boy. Let 'em help ya!"

Finally, Fergie got ahold of Luke Boy's life preserver and tugged it to the side of the boat. Maury fastened one end of a rope and lowered it. Luke Boy came scampering up and stood still, shivering, with his hands in the air.

Fergie waved the hands down. She put a blanket around his shoulders and led him toward the cabin, where Al waited.

When they brought him into the room, Luke Boy's sandy hair was matted to his forehead in a swirl, and his teeth were chattering.

"You okay, boy?" the captain asked.

The wet, shivering deckhand nodded, glancing at the gun in Al's hands.

"Don't fret none," the captain said. "Why don't you go make us a pot of coffee, and if a little o' the brandy spills into your mug, no one's the wiser."

"Is there any food in the galley?" Maury asked. "It seems forever since we ate or were in the mood to do so."

"Nope," the captain said. "There's no galley, just a place by the sick bunk where we can make coffee. We never eat till we get back to shore. The rest of the time, we're too busy shrimping. Well... used to be."

"What about those two mercenaries in the brig?" Al asked. "Should we just heave them over the side, the way they were treating others?"

"It ain't in me to do that," the captain said. "You can do what you please. I'm gettin' used to people shoving me around."

"We'll leave them down there," Al said. "Cold-blooded murder's not in me either."

As Luke Boy went out, Fergie started to follow but not before she patted Al on the shoulder. "I'm glad you're doing the humane thing. It means you're a cut above the sort we're dealing with."

He gave a half shrug. Al couldn't imagine leaving the poor fellow out alone in the gulf, even if he'd been one of the bad ones. Or for that matter, he couldn't stomach throwing living men into the cold gulf. That made him different from them, which was a good thing.

"I sure wish we could call and check on Bonnie." Fergie glanced up at the broken radio. "Or call for some kind of backup." Then she was out the door.

Maury came into the wheelhouse. "I would have tried to reach Bonnie on one of their cell phones, but apparently, no one had any, even those armed guys."

"They're not allowed on the shrimp boats," the captain said. "At least lately. It's a rule. They probably threw yours overboard. That's their usual thing."

"Who's this?" Maury nodded toward the captain.

The captain glanced at Al then Maury. "My name's Abel Barkins. They been Barkins runnin' shrimp boats outta Port Dexter as long as anyone can tell."

"Should we call you Abe?" Maury asked.

"Barky will do, unless you're buying a round. Then you can call me whatever you damn well please."

Al was surprised at how the man's attitude had changed since they'd fished his first mate out of the gulf. "How did a man like you come to have anything to do with whatever's going on with your shrimp boat?" he asked.

"Oh, I'm not supposed to talk about that, and if I was, it's not like I had a helluva choice."

"Wouldn't you rather be shrimping?"

"Humpf. I'd rather they *was* any shrimp. You know I have to fetch in a minimum of a thousand bucks' worth of shrimp a day to break even? Most times these days, I struggle to do that. I gotta fish longer, and we catch fewer."

"What's the problem?" Maury asked.

"*Problems* is more like it. The shrimp is smaller than ever before, and they're way overfished. Then you got all this enviromonster chatter 'bout turtles and bycatch. Everbody's down on the little shrimper, and they's even more of them crowdin' the already-crowded gulf. Meanwhile, the big boys, those hundred-plus-foot offshore trawlers, go out and stay for weeks and come in with the shrimp already froze and ready for market. I got a little boat, by today's standards."

"I see," Maury said.

"The hell you do," Barky said. "And then there's those damn shrimp farmers. More shrimp that hit the market come from them than from us these days, and it's gonna get worse."

"Aren't they more sustainable?" Maury asked.

Barky's head snapped toward him, and he looked like he wanted to spit. "There's those damn imports too. Most folk don't even know where they shrimp is from. The last shrimp you ate probably came from Asia or South America, not from the belly of my piddly boat."

"Still, how does that justify what you're up to here?" Al asked. "Are you saying you condone what you've been doing instead?"

"Hell no. But like I said, I got no other choices."

"Who's running all this?" Al asked. "Someone must be in charge."

"You know I can't say, and I won't say. I ain't happy about it, but it is what it is."

"And what is that?"

"Can't say."

"And the other townspeople, the community, are okay with what's going on?"

"Most everbody is doing better than ever, at least better than before. Any who squawked didn't squawk long."

Realizing he'd gotten all he was going to get from the captain, and even that had been a little more than he'd expected, Al turned to Maury. "What do you think's going on in Port Dexter?"

Maury was looking at the captain but spoke to Al. "I think they're bringing in young girls, way too young of a bunch of girls. They have them cruising the bars and turning tricks in the motels. But that's just the bait on the hook. The worst and most heinous of it is that there's an absolutely fatal honey trap going on. With all the area cops on the payroll, they pick through all the men that come to town and cull out the single ones, those who didn't tell anyone they were sneaking off to the town. They take their vehicles and any money they can, and auto parts are at an all-time high. While the cars, trucks, and SUVs are at the chop shop, the guys are dumped far enough out in the gulf that they're chum. No trace of them can be found. The boats that bring the young girls in may bring other stuff, too, but maybe not if they don't want the DEA sniffing around. There's almost certainly some money laundering going on. Just the stuff we know about is enough to blow a whistle, if we had a whistle."

Al glanced again at the broken ship-to-shore radio. "And you just go along with all this?" he asked Barky.

"You know I can't say nothin.'"

"If you did?"

"Then it'd be me out there feedin' the crabs with my toes."

"I suspect all this has a time window," Al told Maury. "It has to generate a mass of money quickly then shut down and move on before too many people smell something bad in the air."

"It must be big bucks for a while, enough for the risk," Maury said. "Although right now, it doesn't seem risky when everything's running smoothly. And by smoothly, I mean I was almost gargling with the groupers."

"I wouldn't be surprised if drugs were in the mix somewhere too," Al said. "Anyone who can shrug off human trafficking, wholesale grand theft auto, a mountain of felonies, and who makes enough to corrupt a city and county's law enforcement must be hauling it in."

"We need to let someone know and as soon as possible. I wish I could at least get ahold of Bonnie." Maury fidgeted, putting his weight first on one foot then on the other.

Al took a deep breath. They were okay for the moment, but he didn't think they were out of the woods yet, not even back to land. He wished the captain hadn't taken out the radio, but at least the compass worked. They seemed to be headed in the right direction.

He looked back at Barky. "What will you do with those men handcuffed in the brig?"

"Turn 'em loose when we get to shore."

"That's it? Even after you saw them shoving live men off into the gulf to die a probably pretty horrible death?"

"I'm not like them. Don't want to be like them. What about you? Did you ever kill a man?"

"I was in the military in an active war zone, so yes." Al didn't mention the men killed in the line of duty while he'd been in the sheriff's department or the ones who'd come after him or members of his family.

He still managed to get to sleep most nights, since it had been them or him.

But the comparison gave him something to think about as well as a new way of looking at Barky, Luke Boy, and other townspeople who'd been swept along and made to comply with something they knew to be evil.

He shuddered and looked out across the water.

Fergie might have sensed some of what was going through his mind. She stepped closer and put an arm around his waist.

Chapter Fourteen

Bonnie stopped at a traffic light and tried to call Maury again. She got no answer. Then she tried Al and Fergie until the car behind her honked for her to go.

She eased off the brake and went through the intersection. Despite all the excitement, Little Al was asleep in his car seat fastened in place behind her, on the side where she could glance back his way. At least Patty Belle had scooted close beside him, where she could tend to him while Bonnie drove.

Ahead on her right, a small motel appeared, a mom-and-pop sort called Cactus Candle, which likely wasn't part of a chain. The lit blue neon sign said the place had vacancy. She eased off the highway and pulled into the parking lot, within sight of the motel office's picture window. She turned off the engine but didn't get out of the car. She was plumb tired but edgy, too, and knew she would never be able to rest or sleep.

She pictured herself in a room there, pacing back and forth, flipping the television on and off again. *What would I be waiting for? A miracle to happen?*

She dialed Maury's number again—nothing.

She tried Fergie then Al—the same.

Tanner turned from looking out the passenger window to stare at her.

"Yeah, it looks like it's just you, Patty Belle, and me to the rescue, old fellow. It won't do them any good if we just hole up and wait." She shook her head then turned toward the back seat to sign the same thing to Patty Belle.

"Well, hell." She restarted the engine, which had barely had time to cool. She eased out of the motel's lot and back onto the highway then headed back the way they'd come.

"If they're in any kind of trouble, we have to do something." She talked to the dog while staring ahead, her hands gripping the wheel more tightly.

She wanted to sing or hum, "Here we come to save the day." But her insides were whirring like sixteen squirrels in traffic. She tried to think of anything else, something other than the raw fear bubbling inside her.

"If anything has happened to them... I don't know what we'll do."

She worried most about Maury, but Al and Fergie were part of her family too.

Her secure world—made of quiet days by the lake, cooking and caring for a family—was crumbling around her.

What was worse, she couldn't call the law, especially the so-called law that existed in Port Dexter, or any other department either. She wondered if Maury and the others had just turned off their phones to stay covert. She sure wished they hadn't done so without letting her know, if that was the case. She had no way of knowing what might have happened. Trying to think of anything else, she just clenched the wheel even more tightly and drove.

When she stopped to get gas just outside Port Aransas, she and Patty Belle fed and changed the baby. He was asleep almost as soon as she got him back into his car seat. Patty Belle stayed in the car with him while Bonnie walked Tanner and fretted some more.

As he paused to sniff a bush on a corner, she stooped to pet him and rub his back. "You've saved my bacon a time or two in the past, but I don't know that I can do this with you. My pappy walked me through the woods many a time and taught me to shoot a gun till I can nearly pop a pimple off a flea from a hundred yards. But I don't know that I can take you along. All the risk here belongs to me."

Tanner turned and nuzzled closer, rubbing his neck against hers.

Bonnie shook her head. "Oh, damn you. Well, we'll see. That's all I can promise just now until I figure a few things out, and don't think I haven't a notion or two."

When she stood again, feeling a pop in her knees that didn't make her feel ready to storm castles or wrestle bobcats, she had a clearer idea in her head. She grinned and got a head-snap look from a guy coming out of the gas station's convenience store with a twelve-pack under his arm, and she guessed her smile was probably more of a grimacing leer with a twinkle of trouble in her eyes.

Back at the car, she got Tanner into the front seat but opened the door to the back seat to lean in and have a conversation that quickly turned into a flurry of hands, with Patty Belle shaking her head and Bonnie insisting. Finally, with moisture in her eyes and nose running a little, Patty Belle nodded, no longer smiling but looking determined.

Bonnie got back into the driver's seat and kept them headed back to Port Aransas.

A little over an hour later, she pulled up half a block short of the motel where she and the others had stayed, the one she'd taken off from like a scalded bat out of hell not all that long before. Once out of the car, Bonnie looked around in all directions then waved for Patty Belle to follow.

Carrying the baby in his papoose on her chest and holding Tanner's leash, Patty Belle stayed as close as she could as Bonnie eased closer to the motel, staying as much out of sight as possible, not skulking behind hedges or anything that would call attention to herself but walking slowly and keeping on the other side of the street until she was closer and could slip across.

She only had to look around in front of the room where they'd stayed to have all her suspicions realized.

No yellow police department tape had been stretched to mark a crime scene. Where she had left two bloody bodies, the area was sparkling clean, not one sign of blood. Someone with very professional cleaning skills—the way the mob talked about cleaning skills—had disappeared every sign of those who'd tried to kill her.

She nodded to herself.

In their former quarters, the blinds and drapes had been pulled open. She looked inside and saw no crib. The room was clean and ready to be used once more, preferably by someone who didn't know what sort of shooting had recently occurred just outside.

She stayed close to the walls as she eased toward the motel office, skirting around an ice machine then moving back to hug the paint until she got to the office.

Bonnie peeked first, saw the office was empty, and dashed inside. A little bell rang as the door closed behind her. She flipped the dead bolt closed and crossed the room to slip around behind the registration counter, toward the open door that led to the living quarters behind the office.

"Coming," Mary Doughrety called out from somewhere far inside.

Bonnie slipped close to the wall to stand just out of sight and as close as she could get to the door through which Mary would pass.

As soon as Mary came through, Bonnie moved quickly to put an arm around her and hold her Chief's Special to Mary's ear, pulling back the hammer with her thumb. "How close have you ever been to dying?"

"Um. Um. This has to be the closest." Mary's wide-open eyes swung to Patty Belle, the baby, then Tanner before she went back to staring straight ahead, as if grabbing for her last glimpse of life.

"I want you to believe it. You are that close."

The way Mary swallowed hard was audible.

"Why did you do it?"

"What?"

"Don't even try. Why?"

"I... I... I don't know. I panicked. When they took my motel and gave me this one, I guess I felt I owed them something."

"You don't."

"I know that now."

"You should have thought of it then. Have you heard anything about what happened to my husband and friends?"

"No. I just supposed—"

"That they would be dead by now?"

Mary swallowed hard again. She started to reach up toward Bonnie's gun hand.

"Don't you even, for a second, think I won't pull this trigger. Just stay as still as you can. Do you understand?"

Mary nodded slowly, afraid to move her head.

"You have a chance, an opportunity to make right what you've done. Are you willing to grasp that opportunity?"

Again, Mary nodded in slow motion.

"First rule is you don't call them. Understood?"

"Y-Yes."

"Second rule is you tell me who they are—exactly who they are—and who's in charge."

"I can't do that. They will—"

"Goodbye. It's been nice knowing you." Bonnie pressed the gun barrel harder into Mary's ear.

Mary's head tilted, but the barrel stayed in place. If Bonnie could've pulled the hammer back again, she would have done so. That always made an imposing sound.

"Wait. Wait."

"I'm waiting, but I'm pretty impatient and more than a little twitchy."

"These people came to town, the ones in black and soon the others. We turned around, and all of our regular cops were gone, and the new ones were in place. Then it was the sheriff's department."

"And no one said anything?"

"A few did. They were sorry. Then they were gone. The rest of us kind of learned to shut up. I wasn't around long before I was moved the hell outta there anyway."

"Why call them about us? What made you more loyal to them, some clearly evil people, than to us, strangers who did you no harm and brought business your way?"

"I... I... I don't know. It's like I said. I kind of panicked."

"Do you recognize it as the biggest mistake you ever made?"

"It's pretty big."

"The biggest."

"I'm... I'm so sorry."

"You're only beginning to be as sorry as you're gonna be. Now, here's the really big question. Who's in charge? I mean who's in charge of the whole shebang, at the very top?"

"I can't say. I'm not supposed to ever—"

"I'm squeezing my finger right now. I want to impress upon you that you are one-sixteenth of an inch from being a gory red splatter on the far wall. Am I getting through to you? Do you hear and understand me?"

Bonnie's left hand squeezed harder, too, probably bruising Mary, but she didn't care a whit.

"It's... It's a woman. Her name is Catahoula Cathy Castleton. I never even met her. Those who have seemed pretty shook up. Others that met her aren't around to chatter about it at all."

"But you know where she lives?"

Mary hesitated.

Bonnie pulled the barrel from Mary's ear and fired a shot down into the floor. Tanner and Patty Belle both jumped. The baby woke and started to cry. Tanner pressed against Patty Belle's leg while she fussed with Little Al, trying to calm him.

Bonnie shoved the barrel back into Mary's ear too quickly for the women to move, though the ear had to be ringing like a five-alarm fire truck. The barrel probably felt a little warm.

"Yes. Yes, I know where she lives. But it won't do you much good. She has a small army of those assholes in black."

"You let me worry about them."

"Well, you should," Mary said, quivering in Bonnie's tight grasp. "You should tremble to the tips of your toes."

"I don't have a choice. But there is something you're going to do for me."

"What's that?"

Bonnie spun Mary around and put the gun barrel in her other ear. She leaned in closer and gave Mary her most intense glare, which made Mary move her head back.

"What?" Mary repeated.

"You're going to watch Patty Belle and my baby."

"I couldn't."

"I'm not asking. You're gonna. You gotta. I've got no other options. But nothing is going to happen to them, is it?"

"Well, I—"

"Nothing. Right?"

"Yeah. Right." Mary's eyes were as wide as they could get, and she moved her head back another half inch, but Bonnie's gun followed the movement and stayed lodged in Mary's ear.

"'Cause if you squeal on us again or do anything—and I mean any-thing—that causes harm to come to my baby or Patty Belle, I will come back, and what I will do to you will make anything that Port Dexter bunch could do to you look like a party at the beach. Do you under-stand?"

"Um. I—"

"Do you understand?" Bonnie shouted as loudly as she could. "Whatever you can imagine those dudes doing to you, I'll do ten times worse."

Patty Belle and Tanner both flinched. The baby cried harder. Patty Belle tried to rock him quiet.

"Yes." Mary lowered her head and stared at the floor.

"Are you sure you understand everything I've said and what I'll do?"

"Y-Yes."

"You don't want to cross me, or you're going to think those jaspers in Port Dexter are puppy dogs." Bonnie gave her grip with her left hand a little twist. "Say it!"

"P-P-Puppy—" Mary broke into deep, gasping sobs.

Perhaps seeing the bodies Bonnie had plugged and left behind the last time helped Mary Doughrety to get Bonnie's message and believe she was the one to worry about right then. That was good. Bonnie didn't like leaving Little Al or Patty Belle behind, but she had damned little choice. In their little sign language chat in the car earlier, Patty Belle had promised to do all she could to protect and take care of the baby.

Bonnie took the leash from Patty Belle and went down on one knee to face the girl. Neither could sign a word. They pressed their foreheads together. Then Bonnie rose and turned to go.

Bonnie made her way through the motel office and opened the dead bolt on the door. A businessman in a white shirt and a tie was standing there, trying to look peeved at not being able to get right into the office. As late in the day as it was, he probably had a complaint of some kind he wanted to air.

"Entrer," she said, using up what tiny bit of French she knew.

She gave him a half bow and waved him inside, sharing what she thought was a hearty smile. But whatever determined glimmer of Halloween he saw in her face made his eyes open wider. He took a step back and let her and the dog pass.

"C'mon, Tanner." She headed out to Fergie's car. "It's just you and me for now."

Even as she walked away, being apart from Little Al for the first time ever made her heart tug at her, and she wanted to just go back and pull him into her arms. But Maury might or might not be dead, as well as Al and Fergie. She had to try. She might be all they had.

She figured if anyone could help, she could. Those men in the skull masks who had come after her at the motel earlier had found out. They were gone, as if they had never existed. She could have told them, "You're only as fast as the bullet you can get out of the end of your gun." She'd been half a step faster, with no hesitation.

Chapter Fifteen

In the distance, the white aura of the town's lights glowed against the black of the sky, an occasional red or green beam lower along the coastline as they approached the shore. Al had mixed feelings about coming back to Port Dexter and would rather have made for Port Aransas. But Barky had pointed out how low on fuel they were. He would barely be able to make it back to his dock. Al had checked the fuel gauge himself, since he no longer believed a single word anyone associated with the whole Port Dexter mess said, including "and" and "the." Barky might seem a good old salt who'd just been swept along in what was going on, but he'd nevertheless seen a damned lot and done damned little. Al suspected the whole town had a bit of that, those who hadn't bucked and were removed. The situation was as ugly a slice of life as he'd ever come across. All he wanted was to get to a phone and blow a whistle as loudly as he could.

As the taste of salt swept in with a bit of breeze, he found himself savoring being on the water in spite of everything. While the boat steadily neared the shore, the slap of waves against the hull as they rose and fell held a soothing regularity. He wondered for a second or two what a life on the gulf would've been like instead of his years as a sheriff's department detective. However, one or two really horrific storms probably would've squeezed the joy out of that picture and made him glad to be a landlubber.

While they were still a ways out, a thought crossed Al's mind. He took the AR-15s they'd gotten from the two mercenaries on board and dropped the guns over the side of the boat. They were instantly out of sight, sinking a good hundred feet or more, hopefully far enough out that no one could come across them until they'd rusted into useless hunks. As much as he, Fergie, and Maury might need to defend themselves if they were to get clear of Port Dexter, he didn't fancy their chances if they were caught walking the streets while carrying semiautomatic firearms. Fergie nodded as he came back to the helm to join her, Maury, and Barky.

As they got closer and closer to land, Al could make out the masts of ships, the shapes of buildings, and a wider variety of lights—yellows, reds, greens, blues, and bright white.

The water around their boat was a choppy black. Lines of white light stretched out across the moving waves to sway in place on the surface.

The boat rocked into a steady wallow as the outriggers were lifted.

Al didn't see anything like a reception committee of bent cops or anyone else waiting. Maybe they could get off clear and make a run to get out of the blasted town.

Luke Boy stood ready with a rope in hand to leap to the dock and tie the boat into place.

"You see? I got you to land okay, now, didn't I?" Barky stood as he slowed the boat and eased it into place. One arm was still held down by the chain and handcuffed to his chair, but he could steer with one hand.

"You did. But you would have stood by and watched while we were tossed overboard if this had gone another way."

"I told you. I ain't got any choice in the matter."

"Everyone has choices," Fergie said.

"I s'pose Luke Boy made a choice when he jumped overboard the way he did." Barky's mouth twisted up at the corner with sarcasm as he spoke.

"He did," Fergie agreed, "and he's lucky it turned out the way it did for him, and he got fished out before hypothermia set in."

"I s'pose," Barky said but with no sarcasm.

Al nodded. "People who are up to no good are a problem. But those who stand by and do nothing are in some ways just as culpable."

"Culpable?" Barky asked.

"To blame."

The captain shrugged. "No choice is no choice, far as I see it."

Al nodded to Maury, who stepped closer and unlocked the cuff from Barky's hand.

"Thank ye." Barky reached to rub the wrist while keeping the vessel on course.

The boat moved between the lighted red and green buoys, slowing as it neared the docks and the brighter white lights that made lines out across the rippling water.

Birds flapped about in the air, unseen when lost in the dark night sky.

"Ready, Luke Boy?"

"Ready." The first mate stood with the end of a rope in both hands.

Al knew with a boat that size, the captain had to factor in any current, the wind, and the water conditions around the dock they were approaching.

Barky eased the boat alongside and touched the fenders on its side with the lightness of a feather. Luke Boy was in the air and on the dock, cleating off the first rope, and was as quickly back on board and had the second docking rope. In seconds, the boat was secured.

"I expect a peppy time with a lot of explaining to do," Barky said, "but if I was y'all, I would be springing onto that dock and moving your feet briskly."

Without waiting for Luke Boy to set up a gangplank, Al gauged the gap between the boat and dock and took a leap. Fergie and, finally, Maury hopped onto the dock.

"Having second thoughts about not bringing along those AR-15s?" Fergie asked.

Al shook his head. "All we've got to do is keep moving until we've found a phone and made a call or two. We're not clear of anything yet, and this town is as frosty a one as I've seen in many a moon."

The streets near the docks were dark, nothing like the glitter of the bars along the main strip. A rat came out from behind a trash barrel, saw them, and skittered into the night with nearly a whipcrack of its tail.

They went around a corner two blocks away, where they'd parked the borrowed Jeep Cherokee. An empty parking space was where it should have been.

"Well, damn," Al said.

"I guess we've got to shift to a plan B and wing it." Fergie kept her voice low.

Al nodded, wishing he knew the streets better. He'd been to Port Aransas a number of times but never before to Port Dexter. They would pretty much have to follow the lights and figure their way out.

He would have liked to stop and savor the moment, glad to be free, glad to be alive. But they had to keep going as quickly as possible. Their heels clicked on the sidewalks, and he thought he heard faint echoes of each step.

The streets near the docks were mostly in shadow, and they stayed in the darkest of those, keeping close together.

Al was forming a rough plan in his head: find a vehicle and get out of town—as simple as that.

They went around a corner of an older brick building, and spotlights lit up, harsh and glaring in their faces. Al squinted and could see uniforms—not police uniforms but ones like he'd once worn in his early years on the sheriff's department. He could also see guns pointed at them.

As his eyes adjusted, he heard the person in the center say, "Put your guns down on the ground... slowly."

The sheriff's department operating within the city limits—as that close to the docks surely was—meant they were on the same twisted team as the police and not to be trusted at all. Al knew their chances were zero in any kind of shoot-out. As he and Fergie lowered their pistols to the sidewalk, he could make out the uniforms more clearly. The man standing in their center had gold braid around his hat, which matched his gold badge. His nameplate read Sanderson. Al figured him for the sheriff, though his being up in the middle of the night seemed odd.

To the sheriff's left, one of the three deputies with him was doing a damned poor job of suppressing a shit-eating grin. The sheriff nudged him with an elbow, and the grin went away. They were not real cops, which meant they were twice as dangerous and not there to rescue Al and the others.

The deputies moved in and jerked them around to handcuff their wrists behind their backs, patted them down, and checked their pockets. They found only the handcuff key Maury had tucked away. The way they went about it told Al those guys had never been to an academy. They were mere thugs in borrowed uniforms. But the whole damned town seemed to be that way.

Neither Fergie nor Maury had said a word. They exchanged glances as they were led not toward the two sheriff's department cruisers across the street but to the side door of a warehouse. Al didn't see a glimmer of hope on either of their faces, nor did he have any himself at the moment. The hands pinching his upper arms as they led him along were unnecessarily firm. He didn't worry about getting bruises, but Fergie and Maury were being handled as roughly.

Inside, one of the deputies flipped a switch, and a row of overhead fluorescent tubes came on, lighting the nearly empty interior of the building. Only one low row of carefully packed crates lined the far wall. Apparently, someone was getting ready to move or had stored some stuff in the boxes so that they could be readily scooped up if they had to take off.

The deputies lined the three of them up in the center of the hollow space, so at least they weren't against a wall where they were to be gunned down.

Sheriff Sanderson took out his cell phone and made a call.

All Al could think about was getting his hands on that phone and making a call himself.

BONNIE ARRIVED AT THE address Mary had coughed up for Catahoula Cathy's residence. After driving slowly past the tall surrounding wall and main gate of iron, maybe steel, she caught a glimpse of a mini mansion up the hill. "Here we are," she said to Tanner, who was up on his hind legs, looking out the passenger window.

She drove along a wooded area beside the road. After a couple or three more estates, she spotted a short, little-used lane to her left that went into the vegetation far enough to hide Fergie's car. She got a small flashlight out of the glove box and looked for Fergie's gun. It wasn't there. Bonnie knew how many shots she'd fired back at the motel and how many bullets were left—not many—and she had no way of getting more ammo.

She felt around under the seat and finally pulled out Fergie's nightstick, left over from her early days as a cop before she became a detective. She probably kept it handy in case some road rage boiled over or something of the sort. It had a nice heft and would have to do for the moment.

Holding the nightstick and with her Chief's Special shoved under her belt, Bonnie put on Tanner's leash and said, "We hoof it from here."

Years of coon hunting at night with her pappy had taught her how to see at night almost as well as the hounds. She had no need to turn on the flashlight as they crossed the road and worked their way back to Catahoula Cathy's estate.

She lifted Tanner over a stone wall that rose nearly to her chest. Then she had a helluva time scrambling over while still holding on to the leash. They stayed away from any lights and soon came to the ten-foot wall surrounding the place. She peeked through at a rusty, thick-barred metal gate wrapped in thick chains locked by a couple of padlocks.

"Yep. Trip wires and the works, Tanner," she whispered. "I could turn you loose to maybe set off a laser beam alarm and see who responds, but I already know there are probably several of those mercenary gazoonies guarding the place. I gotta figure out a way to get in there that doesn't involve running into any of them."

Bonnie heard a low growl in Tanner's throat at the same time a small twig snapped. She spun around and saw a single guard in a black uniform labeled Security, sneaking along the fence toward her. He held a pistol in one hand pointed in her direction.

When she dropped the leash to pull out her gun with one hand and hold the nightstick with the other, Tanner shot across the open space and, with a fierce growl, leaped at the man, climbed up his combat vest, and went for his throat.

While the man reeled back, trying to knock Tanner away, Bonnie rushed forward as quickly as she could. Before the guy could hit or shoot at Tanner, she swung the nightstick as hard as she could. A pro baseball player might have said he was swinging for the cheap seats, really trying to get his bat's sweet spot on the leather. Her swing had the same effect, making a loud *thunk* as the nightstick landed on the man's temple.

His eyes went blank, and his arms lowered. She was already swinging again. *Thunk!*

The guy crumpled to the ground, dropping his gun.

"At ease!" Bonnie pulled Tanner away from the guy. "We'd better skedaddle."

She had to hold Tanner back with one hand as she bent to pick up the man's gun, a standard police-issue Smith & Wesson .38, Model 15 with a four-inch barrel. "Oh goody. He's using the same ammo as us." She took bullets out of the black leather gun belt and replaced the spent shells from her Chief's Special before shoving the pistol back into her belt. Then she took the rest of the shells and shoved them into her pockets. The guy still wasn't stirring. As she reached for his walkie-talkie, she got a good look at his face.

"It's that Mendlemann guy, one of those first two cops we met on the beach," she whispered to Tanner. "He wasn't very nice to us then, so I feel less bad about knocking him cross-eyed like I did. Now, come on. Let's go."

She let Tanner have his lead as they headed back to the car, and she had to break into a run with her stubby legs to keep up with him. He was a goer when on a mission. Maybe he sensed they were off to save Al, who had once saved him.

Bonnie wasn't even sure Al, Maury, and Fergie were still alive, but she had to keep believing and trying.

She let Tanner into the car then climbed in. At a loss as to what to do next, she was driving toward the front of the estate again when, far ahead, three black SUVs with windows tinted black came out the front gate in a tight formation. They whooshed down the road.

The front gate was just closing as Bonnie drove past it.

"Hang on, Tanner," she said. "We've got our first lead that anything's happening. We'd better not lose those vehicles. But Lordy, look at them go."

She stepped on the gas to keep the mini caravan of black vans in sight.

FERGIE HAD BEEN STANDING up straight long enough that she would've welcomed the chance to sit down. But the sheriff and his thug fake deputies seemed to be waiting for something.

She was thinking that a sheriff had to have been elected, so maybe someone had turned the one in place to the dark side. Or maybe the whole thing, whatever was going on, had been set up a good while back and had only come together more recently, to start the money pouring in through prostitution, auto theft and parts sales, and human trafficking, for all she knew. She hadn't had time to figure exactly what was being done and by whom, and knowing wouldn't even get them out of their current fix, which looked as dark as it could get, probably fatally so.

Fergie glanced at Al, wishing she could squeeze his hand.

She figured out what they had been waiting for when two fake cops came in to replace the fake deputies. She tensed when she recognized one of them, Furbister, who seemed to be staring at her as he came across the empty space to them.

"Well, well, well," he said. "We meet again. How I thought of you over those long years in prison, Detective Ferguson. The things I wanted to do to you, and here you are, practically served up on a plate. Hmm. Hmm. Hmm." He rubbed his hands together.

But all of them just stood there, occasionally glancing toward the door.

"Who are we waiting for?" Fergie asked. "Someone important?"

She thought she heard his teeth grind before he answered. He sure was wound tight. But getting under his skin wouldn't give them any kind of advantage and might just hurry things along.

Furbister started to pace as the other cop stood still and watched. Furbister caught himself and stopped. He moved in front of Fergie, who was starting to think she'd been standing for a very long time.

"Do you know anything 'bout Louisiana?" he asked.

"Hey. *Tsk. Tsk. Tsk.*" The other cop held a hand up.

"It don't matter none." To Fergie, Furbister said, "You see, we ain't supposed to talk about it. But you know. What happens in Davy Jones's locker stays in Davy Jones's locker."

"You saying I might die soon?" Fergie asked.

"There's no 'might' about it." That seemed to give Furbister a special joy, and his face broke into a broad grin.

Fergie swallowed and didn't have a snappy comeback.

"Them Louisiana folk think highly of a dog they have there, the Catahoula Leopard Dog, what was trained to work in swamps. It's strong, it's loyal, and it has a higher energy level than a pit bull. Hell, some of them swamp folks swear a Catahoula can make a pit bull wet its pants."

"All very interesting," Fergie said, "but how's—"

"'Cause you're fixin' to meet the one and only Catahoula "Cat" Cathy Castleton... in person, and that's a one-time event in a person's life. Now, how cool is that?"

"Not cool at all," Fergie would have answered, but they were interrupted by four men in black combat gear, not wearing masks but carrying AR-15s as they entered the warehouse. They spread out, looked around, then focused on the door.

A woman came through. Fergie felt a twinge of disappointment, even though she should've been fretting about her life.

Fergie had expected a slender, dark-haired woman in a black leather outfit, looking like that woman who wanted to make a coat out of Dalmatians, Cruella de Vil. Instead, she faced a stout, almost matronly blond woman in the sort of red business pantsuit one might wear while selling real estate. The shoes looked like Prada or Gucci, something outside Fergie's interest and price range. But the woman had no smoldering cigarette holder or squinting stare. She did notice that Cat's hair looked like she'd just come from a hair salon, probably having gotten the blond touched up too.

Cat caught her looking. "You're wondering something. The answer is yes, I do keep a full-time hair dresser on my staff. She also does nails and helps with the cleaning."

That figures. Fergie couldn't imagine someone like Cat having to sit and wait for her turn at a regular beauty salon.

She strolled toward them but stayed a dozen feet away.

Fergie noticed that all the gun barrels were pointed toward them. She swallowed hard again.

Cat turned to Furbister. "And as for you, haven't you heard that bit about loose lips sinking ships?"

Furbister blushed, as tough as he was. "I was... I was just—"

"Save it for your memoirs." She spun on her heel and stared at Al. "I just wanted to see who was causing the ripple in my pond before I sent them out to play in the gulf again. Unfortunately, we can't use Barky's boat this time, as he is getting his radio fixed."

"Why not kill them here and then haul the bodies to the boat?" Furbister asked.

"Do you want to do the clean-up?"

"No."

"Then take them to the boat." Cat turned back to Fergie, Al, and Maury. "Everything here is carefully orchestrated. You petty people are messing with that, affecting my schedule. It's only fair that you pay the ultimate price." The woman shifted her stance, bending closer to give them an intense stare. "Now, what I want to know from y'all is what made you want to come down here and mess in my bidness."

Fergie didn't buy the sudden shift to the patois of a street person. Though she was sure Cat had dealt with that sort, she was probably more comfortable around the set that lifted a little finger while raising a tea cup—in between killing people, that was.

But the threat was real—very real.

From the corner of her eye, Fergie could see Maury shaking, his lips pressed tight. Al simply stared ahead like a prisoner of war. She was pretty sure he'd never been taken prisoner during his military stint, but he was stoic and firm.

Cat glanced from one of them to the other, finally settling on Fergie. "I don't know whether to call you a string bean or a tall drink of water. Why don't you help me understand."

Fergie thought of one or two zippy things to say about a woman who was at least a head shorter. She bit her tongue to keep from saying anything at all.

"Well, hasn't this been a splendid waste of time." Cat shrugged and turned to two of the men in black. "Take them away."

Fergie was keeping up as brave a face as she could but felt one stupid tear trickle down a cheek. That got part of a smile out of Cat, who spun and started for the door, her other security guards and the fake cops following closely.

As they were led out the door by the two armed men in black, Fergie took in a deep breath of the night air, which still held a rich hint of salt from being so close to the sea. The sky was black, with no sign of stars or moon. The streetlights were far enough away that everyone was walking in shadows.

She was trying very hard not to think about that night being her last one alive. But one thing about having long, lanky legs was that when her knees wobbled, they really wobbled. She had to slow herself to take steady steps. The guy behind her prodded her with his gun.

Push all you want, she thought, *but I'm in no hurry to die.*

Chapter Sixteen

With every step they took, Al was calculating any possible moment of opportunity. Just a glimmer—that was all he was asking for—but nothing came. They were three unarmed people being herded along by two heavily armed ones.

They left the sidewalk, and their shoes clicked as they walked on the wooden boards running along the docks. One of the shrimp boats waited ahead. Even at that late hour, birds were rising around it. A breeze blew in off the sea, cool and salty but not hopeful.

If he dove sideways into the water, he would be abandoning the others. Even then, handcuffed as they were, swimming would be hard, and he'd probably be shot within seconds of hitting the water. He had to bide his time and hope.

Still deep in thought, he heard a loud wooden *thunk*.

He spun in time to see the mercenary who'd been behind him, covering them with a gun, fall sideways into the water. Where he'd been walking, feisty Bonnie stood, lowering a nightstick.

The guard nearest Al turned and lifted his AR-15 toward Bonnie.

Al kicked the side of the man's knee as hard as he could. The guy crumpled to his left but was still standing and trying to lift his rifle as quickly as he could.

Fergie stepped forward to kick hard at the other knee.

Al kicked again. As the man started to fall, Bonnie rushed forward between them and bashed the mercenary on a temple with her full weight behind the nightstick. Al bent and grabbed the dropping weapon, catching it just as the man splashed into the water.

Bonnie's cell phone flew out of her pocket to plop into the water right after the man.

"Oh, blast and bother," she said, touching the pocket where it had been.

"You did quite a job on them with that nightstick," Fergie said. "Did you ever play Little League as a kid?"

"Nah, but I gotta admit I fear I'm startin' to get more than a little addicted to hearing the sound that nightstick makes on bad guy heads," Bonnie said. "It's like thumping coconuts in spring."

"People enjoy themselves in whatever way they can," Fergie said to lighten the moment. She was still breathing hard, probably thinking about how close they'd come to heading back out into the gulf.

Handcuffs were still pinching Al's wrists, so they weren't all the way clear yet. Bonnie handed Maury a bobby pin while they all moved over to look down into the water. No one was swimming about, nor were bubbles coming up, but the steady lap of waves was coming in to press up then down along the wooden pilings.

The night seemed quiet, and they had it all to themselves. No alarm was sounding from the direction of the warehouse.

Maury had his handcuffs off and started on the others. In seconds, Al and Fergie's hands were free as well. Fergie was rubbing her wrists.

"Come on. We'd better shuffle off to Buffalo," Bonnie said.

"Where's—"

Before Fergie could finish the question, Bonnie said, "Tanner's in the car. Your car, by the way. I had to leave Little Al and Patty Belle... with someone for a spell."

A burr in her voice showed enough emotion that Fergie didn't ask her anything else.

"Let's go," Bonnie said.

She'd been clever enough to park the car out of sight, a couple of blocks away from where she'd followed the black vans to the warehouse.

A fight began in the back seat while Al was still fastening his safety belt in the driver's seat before even having turned the key. He'd known it was coming when he heard Bonnie and Maury muttering back and forth as they were heading to the car.

"I can't believe you left Little Al with *that* woman, the very one who ratted us out to this Cat lady. And poor little Patty Belle too."

"I had to save you guys, and I did," Bonnie said. "There were no babysitters available or day care centers open in the middle of the night for me to turn to, if I even knew where to go and ask in a town I'm not from. You gotta know this is chewing at me far more than what's going on in your bony head. I'm sick about it, just plain sick, and I want us to be done and outta here so I can go and scoop up my little boy in my arms and never let go."

That shut Maury up.

"We've got two things going for us," Bonnie said. "They don't know about this vehicle, and they may not know we've gotten away... yet."

Al nosed the car to the corner, still a block away from the main strip, where he'd pictured them making a getaway. A police car with flashing blue and red lights went whooshing by in one direction. After hardly a pause, a black SUV roared by, going the other way.

"I'm betting those fake cops we first met at the beach ran the plates on my car," Fergie said. "It's why we put it in storage."

"And I think the alarm has properly sounded on us getting away," Al said.

"It wasn't from those two guys who're in the water," Maury said.

"I wish we'd have had a chance to check them for cell phones," Al said.

"I kind of popped one guy on the head over at Cat's mansion," Bonnie said, "and it was a guy we'd met earlier in a cop's uniform that time we were at the beach. I'm betting he had a major complaint when he came to and felt for a lump."

"Putting aside how the alarm happened, it seems pretty clear that a hunt is on," Fergie said.

On her lap, Tanner pressed against the side window, eager to try to look out and see.

Al eased to the corner until he could look up and down the main strip. The lights from the Bent Fox's Tail, Gnarly Gus, and Bayou Bunny were beckoning in full neon brightness. The yellow light from the streetlights lit up the main drag until it was like daytime so that none of the men leading their much younger female companions to a motel might stumble or lose their way.

A police motorcycle went by on a cross street a block away, then the main street was clear for the moment.

Al shot across, wishing he had a map of the city. Like most towns along the Gulf Coast, Port Dexter had probably grown up all higgledy-piggledy, and the streets went every which way, like the cowboy who hopped on his horse and rode off in all directions.

They were barely across the main drag when the first raindrops hit the windshield. In seconds, it was a downpour and not just an everyday downpour but a real frog-walloper of a storm that would clear out the drains and sweep leaf litter along and soon form puddles and little rivers along the curbs.

"This is a good thing," Al said.

"Do you think it'll give us enough cover to get clear of this town?" Fergie asked.

"I'm hoping."

Al cringed every time he saw one of the pursuing vehicles zip across at a distance. Even in the rain, he felt sure they might get recognized. He'd been involved in a few car chases back in his day, and he didn't fancy their chances of getting away from as many pursuers in cars, motorcycles, and copters as the Cat lady could probably muster. She had a small army and wasn't afraid to use the whole lot of it.

He caught a glimpse of the light bar on top of a police car coming their way without its lights flashing. He made an abrupt right onto an even smaller street then took a sharp left, going past residences and a few businesses. Ahead, a car wash was up a slight hill. He zoomed toward it and slid inside until the car was hugging one cinder block wall.

He glanced back in time to see the police car rush by and heard its loud Interceptor motor slowly fade as it hurried on.

The car wash felt like a good spot, unlikely to be used in the middle of a storm, so Al thought he'd sit there a spell.

Tanner stretched and got up from Fergie's lap to move over and sit on Al's and let him scratch him behind the ears. Al couldn't tell if Bonnie was sobbing quietly and didn't want to ask. Maury had moved closer to put his arms around her.

"There are three basic directions out of a town like this, where south only goes out into the gulf," Al said after a few minutes. "I'll try to check them without getting spotted. If that doesn't work, maybe some smaller street or road works. We can hardly sit here and wait for daylight. There'll be no hiding then."

Al stayed on back streets, heading in the general direction of where they'd come into town. The heavy rain helped as a cover but wasn't perfect. A couple of times, he had to swing off the street they were on, and once, he drove into someone's driveway, where a square-cut hedge hid them as a police car went by.

When he knew he had to get over to the main street to get out of town, he peeked then zipped across. His glance toward the way out told him all he needed to know as a row of blue and red lights flashed around and around. The steady rain made the lights look like the glitter of gems, but that way looked far from inviting.

"A roadblock," Maury said from the back seat. "Do you think all the ways out are blocked?"

Al didn't want to answer, but his gut knew. He was doing a little mental math at the same time. Given all the men it would take to maintain roadblocks and all the men scrambling around in police cars and black SUVs, he knew that Cat woman had a lot of staff, and that kind of skilled manpower wasn't cheap.

"She has to be dealing some in drugs too," Fergie said. "Those shrimp boats come in, and they're not carrying just young girls. The trips out may be carrying laundered money."

"Those boxes that were packed and waiting in that warehouse where they took us," Al said. "Do you think they might contain cash that was packed and ready for a split?"

"That's my thought," Fergie said. "That's another plus of having bars, motels, and all that's going on that we haven't even caught a glimpse of yet. It's going to take half a dozen agencies to sort through all of what's happening."

"It's a daring thing to take over a whole town, corrupt it to the core, make a ton of money, and disappear when there's even a hint that you're about to be caught. That's what we represent to them, a danger, the same as Bobby Ray Champion did. We're a whistle that's about to blow before this madwoman is done raking it in hand over fist."

They got near enough to the other end of the town to find it just as roadblocked.

The northern way out was the same: flashing lights and waiting cars. Some of those looked like sheriff's department vehicles.

Al started trying back streets, seeing if he could find any neglected smaller street where they could slip out and around the roadblocks. He always ended up in cul-de-sacs and on streets that looped around to come back onto whatever street he'd been on before.

Frustrated, hungry, and tired, he kept driving, one eye on the gas gauge and the other wary of law enforcement, such as the town had, the kind ready to pounce on them and do anything but play fair.

Then he saw something, slowed, and turned around at the next intersection.

"What did you see?" Fergie sat up straighter in the passenger seat. Tanner caught the mood and pressed his snout closer to the window while peering out.

"This." Al pulled up a driveway.

The two-story house leaned a bit to one side. The upper story's window was broken. Wind and rain had sanded most of the former white paint away until the house was mostly the light brown of bare wood. The wooden garage door had fallen off and lay on the ground. The bushes had grown up into scraggly lumps, and the grass, which hadn't been cut in many a moon, was tall and went in many directions.

"Perfect," Al said.

"Are you thinking of buying?" Fergie asked. "I didn't see a for-sale sign."

"No. But this will be a fine place to hide your car, Fergie, while we get us some new wheels. Are you up to a little grand theft auto, Maury?"

"Only if Bonnie doesn't think I'll make it a standard practice."

"Do you plan to steal some harmless citizen's vehicle?" Fergie tilted her head.

"No. Remember those cars we saw lined up outside that chop shop? They were just waiting to be wheeled inside to become part of a spare parts network sprawling from Kalamazoo to Carmel."

He drove carefully through the town. Squad cars were still lit up and buzzing back and forth through the town. Their lights made them easier for him to spot. On the off chance that somebody was clever enough to turn off the lights and wait, he checked every car parked ahead along the streets they took.

Al stopped a couple of blocks away from the chop shop. "Do you have everything you need?" he asked Maury.

"I wouldn't mind having a Slim Jim to open the doors, but maybe they left them unlocked with the keys in them, since they expect to be chopping them into parts in a short while, certainly before dawn."

He got a hug from Bonnie before heading out into the rainy night. They watched him slide along close to any structure he was near. In moments, he was invisible.

"That's my Maury, a man of many talents."

Five minutes later, a silver Honda Civic came in their direction with Maury behind the wheel. He waved to them. Al turned Fergie's car and headed back to the abandoned house.

Once there, Al got out in the rain to clear out the garage and make sure they didn't puncture a tire on anything. Fergie slid over to the driver's side, and he waved her in.

The rain covered their activities, but Maury kept the lights off on the Civic while he waited. Bonnie, Tanner, and Fergie ducked their heads and hurried over to the car he was driving.

Al struggled for a moment with lifting the wet wooden garage door, and Fergie popped out of the Civic and sloshed back through the puddles and rain to take the other side. They propped it in place to hide the interior of the garage.

All of them were soaked. Tanner added to the joy of the moment by briskly shaking his fur while on Al's lap. That hardly mattered, since Al couldn't get any wetter.

"Where to?" Maury asked.

"To the Batcave, Alfred," Bonnie said.

Al shook his head. "While we have the temporary luxury of being in a vehicle they aren't looking for just now, maybe we can find someplace to buy a burner phone. Lordy, how I miss the days when phone booths were all over the place."

"But we have no IDs and no money or even credit cards," Fergie said.

"I don't know what plan we have, but I hope it happens soon," Maury said. "We have only a quarter of a tank of gas."

"Life is all about challenges." Al petted Tanner's wet fur and tried to think of something, anything.

Their best hope was to get clear of the town to make a call. But the place was like a flypaper that wouldn't let go of him or give him and the others a way out.

CATAHOULA CATHY STOOD in the high cupola of her house on its hill. From there, she could look out across the bit of the planet she'd been able to corrupt utterly, turning it into a stream of money. She couldn't see the streets from where she stood, but she could make out the aura of Port Dexter's lights against the sky. It had all been a smoothly oiled machine and should've gone on being a milkable cash cow for another six months or a year before she would need to disappear as though she'd never been there.

When she had moved in for however brief a stay, the cupola had held an easy chair, a minibar, and a reading lamp. She'd had them removed and replaced with a single folding metal chair. Life was about discipline and drive if she was to succeed big. She'd fibbed to that string-bean redheaded gal about her hairdresser. She had a local come to the house twice a week. That was it.

Someday, she would have one cushy stay-at-home mansion with live-in help. She would have everything she could possibly desire and eat the very best foods until she was perfectly round but not until she'd amassed enough money to compensate for having grown up wearing hand-me-down clothes and being laughed at by the other public-school children. She'd been ashamed of parents who had to work hard at menial jobs and still could only afford meat once a week, and that was chicken on Sundays. School or hard work wasn't the answer for her. She was smarter than that and willing to step on a few heads to get where she wanted to be.

She used to lie in her too-firm twin bed and stare up at a crack and a stain in the ceiling, plotting and conniving. All she had to do was plan carefully, build a set of the right personal skills, and create an algorithm of steps to amass the kind of fortune about which those poor, deluded lottery ticket buyers could only dream.

America used to be the kind of place where a person with ambition and the right kind of hired help could go out and grab gold, oil, or lumber or take over the fur trade the way John Jacob Astor had done. Those days might've been gone, but she had her own way of getting there, and nothing was going to stop her.

She heard footsteps coming up the stairs and turned to face them. One of the men in black combat gear stepped into the glassed-in room. Even in the dim light, she could make out his face as he tugged off his silver-and-black skull mask and held it in one hand.

"What the hell's going on out there, Max?" she asked.

Max Varon was the head of what she called her Demon Dozen—well, eight of them at that point. She'd almost called him Baron Varon at first, but nothing was noble about him, other than how he carried himself, a clear leader among the mercenary riffraff of former Special Forces, CIA, and a couple of other groups for hire to the very rich. They had skills that went beyond personal protection, abilities that included sniping, copter piloting, and exceptional cleaning skills. A little blood or a body or two were always around, which needed their attention.

"Nothing yet," Max said. "We've got everyone looking."

"But not finding?"

"They can't get far."

"It's way too soon to shut down and clear out. But if they get loose, and they find a way to squeak, we may need to do just that. We've never had setbacks like this. We've run this like a smoothly oiled machine in the last two towns." She had enough stashed away in offshore accounts in Switzerland and the Cayman Islands to stop and run. *But from such insignificant pests as these? Never.*

"I've lost four of my best men," Max said.

"They can hardly be your 'best' men if they were taken out by the scruffy lot I saw."

"They were good enough when they weren't getting blindsided."

"Who are these people? They should have been like flies that needed swatting. Who are they?"

"Just flies," he said, "who will soon enough be found and swatted."

Through clenched teeth, she said, "Make it happen."

Chapter Seventeen

"I never checked to see if that security guard I conked on the bean back at Cat's mansion had a cell phone. I could have just used it," Bonnie said. "But I still had a phone of my own then, before it decided to go swimming."

"What'd you just say?" Al asked, glancing in her direction.

"You heard me."

"You're a genius, Bonnie."

"What? Really?"

"That's the only way we can get a phone," Al said. "The stores aren't open, and we have no money if they were. They may even stake out the stores, at that. There's only one no-cost way to get access to a phone. There's risk. But there's reward."

"Plus, that's the last place they'll be looking for us, at her place." Fergie turned to smile back at Bonnie.

"I'm guessing a security guard patrols the perimeter on a regular basis," Bonnie said. "You want I should be the one to conk the daylights outta him? I'm getting kind of good at it... and I'm starting to enjoy it more than I should."

"We'll see." Al glanced at Fergie, who shrugged.

That was okay with her. She'd told him before that she had no special fondness for bonking people on the head, even back when she'd carried that nightstick as part of her rookie cop uniform.

Maury drove out toward Cat's estate, her highly protected sanctum sanctorum, the one place she would feel safest.

"Up ahead, on your left," Bonnie said as Maury drove past the front gate.

"I see we both picked the same spot to stow a car when snooping around out here," Al said as Maury drove down the short lane until the Civic was out of sight.

Al checked the glove box for a flashlight. There was none.

"It's okay. I can see pretty well in the dark. I got the night vision of an owl." Bonnie slapped the end of the nightstick into her open palm. "Now, let's go and thump on some coconuts."

Al bent close to give Fergie a kiss. He patted Tanner's head. Fergie had to hold the dog tightly because he wanted to go too.

"You stay and protect Fergie," Al said, "and she'll protect you. I wish I could leave you a gun."

Bonnie took a cue and bent to give Maury a kiss.

"We should be okay," Fergie said. "You and Bonnie will be on the front line."

Bonnie had her Chief's Special and the nightstick. Al carried the one other gun they had, the AR-15 he'd grabbed from the mercenary who was busy falling sideways into the water.

As soon as they'd scurried across the road, Al looked up at the sky. Scattered clouds moved in irregular patterns that sometimes showed patches of stars and the moon and made for a black sky at other times.

Bonnie was already off at a near jog, heading in the direction of Cat's place.

A few dogs barked in the distance, and lights speared out from the other mini-mansion-sized houses they passed. But they saw no one.

They'd timed the visit to about the same time Bonnie had found Mendlemann patrolling the perimeter of the grounds.

Al liked their chances better when coming up against one of the crooked cops getting in a little overtime as a security guard rather than facing the elite mercenaries in black.

When they neared the gate, they stayed back, hugging the shadows of a cluster of bushes and trees just off the path where the security guard would pass.

The time seemed to crawl. Finally, Bonnie held up a finger. Her ears were sharper than Al's, more fine-tuned to the little sounds of night hunting.

A man was coming, shining a flashlight along the perimeter and sporadically out into the vegetation near the wall.

Al ducked low. Bonnie was already hugging the ground.

As the security guard got closer, Al recognized the man. He was the smaller of the two cops they'd first met at the beach, Adams, although he wore no name tag at the moment, just the security outfit. Yet he still had the face of a weasel with a twist to his mouth that said he was prone to cleverness or meanness.

The guy's light barely missed them in its swing just over their heads. He took a couple more steps, and Bonnie sprang. She put a lot of hips and shoulder and all her body into the swing.

The thud sounded at the same moment the guard's legs went all rubber chicken, and he crumpled onto the path he'd been following.

They both rushed to him and patted him down, searching for a phone. They didn't find one. Al took the guy's pulse. He was alive, but if he'd been a baseball, the hit would probably have been a triple or a homer.

"The guys on the boat said they weren't allowed to have cell phones on them," Al whispered.

"That don't mean they don't sneak one anyway," Bonnie whispered back.

She pulled up the man's pant legs, one after the other. A cell phone was tucked into one of the guy's shin-high black socks. Al grabbed the phone.

Bonnie was busy getting the guard's gun and flashlight. She shined the light on the phone, and Al typed a text message as quickly as he could to his friend Jaime Avila: *Port Dexter. ASAP. Al Quinn.* He hit the send button.

Bonnie held up a finger. "I just heard something."

"Could it be them you heard?" Al nodded to his left.

Four men in black held AR-15s pointed at Al and Bonnie.

Their chances were zero, so Al lowered the gun he held, and Bonnie did the same, even taking the small Chief's Special from her belt when one of the gun barrels waved toward it.

One of the men snatched the cell phone out of Al's hand and looked at the screen. Another of them had bent to gently slap at the cheeks of the fallen security guard.

Their faces were those of hardened mercenaries. Al couldn't think of a thing he could say to them, and they didn't look the sort to encourage conversation anyway.

Al got slowly to his feet and reached down to help Bonnie up. The nightstick fell from her hand with a wooden clatter. Any ray of hope he had was pretty well gone. He could only hope Fergie, Maury, and Tanner could get clear.

FERGIE KEPT GLANCING at her watch. She knew how long Al and she had taken to reach that locked gate in the estate's stone wall. The night was a fairly solid sheet of black around them. Occasionally, she could make out a bit of movement as the wind moved the ends of the vegetation nearby.

She cracked her window to ensure fresh air for Tanner. An owl hooted in the distance. A pair of doves were making their mating calls closer to the car.

"I should have gone along too," Maury said from the back seat.

"You would have just slowed them down and not added much. Bonnie has years of night hunting with her pappy, and Al has a military background. They have as good a chance as anyone. This isn't my pick of a way to get to a phone to make a call, but we could hardly go beating on doors in that town. We wouldn't know who we could trust, or we'd as likely get shot at as a threat to someone's home."

Fergie looked up from her watch and thought she saw a flutter of movement in the black of night around them.

"I'm starting to think, though, that banging on doors or begging for money so we could buy a phone would have been a safer way to go than this, coming right to this Cat lady's place," Maury said.

Fergie tilted her head. She could no longer hear the doves that had been making a steady noise.

Tanner began a low growl in the back of his throat.

Fergie reached for a gun she didn't have.

"Who—" Maury started.

"Shhh."

Their black outfits made them almost impossible to see until they were right up to the car. Four men, holding guns pointed directly at her, surrounded the car.

Tanner growled more loudly and barked. She moved a hand to hold his face and muzzle him. Barking at the men wasn't going to help.

She had a bare second or two to wonder about Al and Bonnie. One of the men was motioning for her to get out of the car. They were the sort of men to open fire if she didn't, so she hooked Tanner up to his leash and unlocked her door.

Fergie held the leash tightly as she got out. Tanner was pulling at it, snarling and trying to get at the men.

"I say we shoot the dog here," one of the men said.

"She said no. But I suppose if it attacks us."

Fergie tightened her grip on Tanner's leash.

The red eyes and reverse lights of one of the black SUVs were backing up toward where they stood.

As they started to climb inside, Fergie saw Al and Bonnie, his wrist handcuffed to hers. Maury slid next to Bonnie and got handcuffed to her.

"Fasten the dog to someone, or we leave it behind," one of the men said.

Fergie fastened one end of the leash to Al's leg above the knee. Then she sat next to him and got her wrist handcuffed to his.

Two of the mercenaries in black crowded in with them, pushing them closer. The rest headed toward another black SUV backing toward them.

"We're having quite a day of it, aren't we?" Al said to Fergie.

"Did you—"

His eyes moved to the nearest guard, who was looking away. He held up a finger.

He'd gotten one call out. Fergie would've liked to savor that one little trickle of hope, but she knew better. Even in a best-case scenario, a rescue would come far too late. She bent to look down the row at Bonnie, whose cheeks were wet. She would be thinking about Little Al having to grow up without her. Maury looked bewildered, not knowing what to think or how to comfort Bonnie.

Only Al looked halfway calm. He was rubbing Tanner's head as a stress reliever, although why the dog had been spared confused Fergie, unless that Cat lady wanted them all to suffer jointly.

Al was looking away, deep in thought. When his head swung her way, she caught a glimmer of intense sadness. They'd just started their life together, had waited all that time to get married only after they were both retired. *Now this.*

She felt a kick low in her gut, and despite her trying to think of almost anything else, a tear trickled down her cheek. Embarrassed, she looked away so that Al wouldn't see.

The SUV's tires rumbled as it pulled onto the road, taking them back into the dark heart of the town they'd so wanted to escape.

Chapter Eighteen

J aime Avila came out of the shower at his gym and rubbed himself with one of the big white towels supplied in stacks on a table at the end of a row of lockers.

He glanced at himself in the mirror—he had a pretty fit body for someone his age, bronze from the sun and his Latino heritage. Some colleagues had described him as being the look and shape of a high-caliber copper-jacketed pistol bullet. He patted his stomach. Only a little of the impact of beer was showing. Even his ex-wife liked to come around from time to time to ride the Tilt-A-Whirl that was Jaime. They couldn't live together, she said but found no reason they couldn't still party now and again.

He tossed the towel aside and began to pull on his clothes, and he took his cell phone out of his pants pocket and glanced at it. Nothing had come from his office, but he had a text message from a number he didn't recognize. He opened it.

Port Dexter. ASAP. Al Quinn.

That was a puzzler. He never heard from Al by text message and hadn't heard all that much since Al retired and got married. The text was out of the blue.

He punched in the number for Shively, the ICE intelligence officer. "Yeah? What's up?"

"You hear anything lately about Port Dexter, down on the coast?"

"No. Quiet as can be for two or three years. Not a peep."

"Isn't that kind of odd for a town on the water?"

"Does seem unusual. Maybe the place is saving up to explode all at once. Why?"

"I think I'm gonna hop down that way with a couple of the guys. Look around."

"Let me know if you find anything. The place has a pretty drab file for the moment as is, especially for a coastal town."

Jaime sent a text to the number from which he'd received the text message: *What's up?*

He got an answer almost immediately: *Nothing. Ignore previous text. Al Quinn.*

That didn't feel right. He tried calling the number back but got no answer.

He called Hank Simonson. "Get us a copter ready. I'll meet you at the hangar. We're going to make a quick hop to the coast. It's probably nothing, but maybe we can score some fresh seafood."

THE MEN IN BLACK ALMOST jerked Fergie off her feet while pulling her out the back doors of the van. She could barely stand. One of her arms was stretched out by the handcuff attaching her to Al's wrist. It bit at her flesh until Al was outside too. Tanner's leash, tied around Al's leg just above his left knee, made it harder for him to move. That didn't keep the mercenaries from yanking him hard to get him out. Tanner had settled into a steady low growl, and Fergie felt like growling also.

Bonnie then Maury was yanked outside too. Only two of the men in black had been in the back with them for the ride, so they were extra rough in horsing the line of prisoners toward the warehouse door.

The driver came around to look up and down the street. Then he stepped closer to give Maury a boot to his rear end. "Keep moving. Get inside."

Tanner snapped a bite of air.

It probably didn't matter if anyone saw them, since their captors seemed to get away with whatever they wanted in town.

They stumbled inside. The worst, for Fergie, was having to hear the usually feisty and scrappy Bonnie steadily sobbing, which had to be about Little Al, even above Maury and the rest of them facing what they were.

Catahoula Cathy Castleton was there, waiting. She was wearing a black business pantsuit with a single strand of medium-sized pearls—no whip or knee-high boots, but that was the aura she was putting out. She stood in the center of the warehouse's empty middle with six of her mercenaries in black lined up around her. She looked angry and impatient.

Fergie thought a few more crates were piled up against the far inside wall of the otherwise large, echoing room. All the men had their hair in buzz cuts, and all were clean-shaven. Earlier, she had seen at least a couple of them wearing tactical combat masks that looked like skulls. None of them felt the need to mask their faces at the moment, which pretty well summed up their expectations for the future of their captives.

Bonnie crumpled to the cement floor, sobbing more loudly. Maury on one side and Al on the other had to go to one knee, but Tanner stopped growling and went over to nuzzle Bonnie and lick at one wet cheek, trying to comfort her.

"Can you shut her up?" Cat snapped.

Bonnie made herself stop sobbing, but that just caused loud hiccups instead. She struggled and, with a little help from Maury and Al, got back to her feet. She looked braver, if a little resigned.

"I'm still checking to ensure that you idiots haven't done more damage than I know about," Cat said. "I'm missing four men from my elite squad, but I'm more concerned about what the rest of the world knows and whether I have to shorten my schedule, consider my losses, and move on. At bottom, you four have been a righteous pain."

Tanner barked.

"The dog too," she said. "It's why I said to bring him along."

Fergie had counted the eight men in black present. She knew what had happened to the missing four. So the Cat woman had probably started with a security team of twelve, a few of whom could fly copters and at least one of whom was a crack sniper. They looked like one tough bunch of heartless hombres.

Cat glanced at her watch. "What's keeping those two?"

Fergie tried to connect with Al's eyes, if only for some sort of goodbye. They were tired, hungry, and apparently barely a speed bump for whatever kind of crime machine the Cat woman was running.

The woman was glaring at him. "Don't worry about that one text message you sent," she said. "We told him not to come."

Al didn't give her the satisfaction of reacting. But Fergie felt another kick in the stomach as her one feeble ray of hope fluttered away. Jaime would probably have been too late anyway, but the frail idea that he might come and start a cleanup of the town had been keeping her standing up straight. Now, her legs felt almost unable to hold her upright.

She tried again to get Al to look her way, but his jaw was clenched tight, his eyes fixed on Cat.

Look at me, dammit, Fergie thought. *Don't let my last glimpse of you in life be the side of your head!*

"Is there anything else I should know about? A message in a bottle or maybe up in a balloon?" Her eyes narrowed.

Al said nothing but just glared back.

"Ah, here they are," Cat said.

Two cops came in the door. One was Furbister. The other was Mendlemann, who had a white bandage around his forehead where Bonnie had beaned him with her nightstick.

Cat stayed fixed on Al. "I think we can assume you had just the one feeble try, and since we spiked that cannon, your meddlesome moment in the spotlight is done here. I think you know what that means." She turned to the two cops. "This time, just kill them here."

"Like I suggested last time," Furbister said.

She glared at him. "Just take care of it."

"Well, send your best cleaners to work their magic while we take the bodies out for chum. Ex-cops are just as apt to bleed as real people, you know."

"You didn't say they were ex-cops."

"It don't matter a hill of beans. At least two of them were. They're retired. I can't speak for the others, and the dog sure as hell isn't K-9 material. This one, Detective Ferguson, is the one who sent me up to prison." He pointed at Fergie.

"You're the one who put yourself in prison," Fergie said. "I was merely the facilitator." She should have kept her mouth shut but figured she wasn't long for the world anyway.

Furbister's face flushed an angry red, and his hands curled into fists as he lunged a half step closer.

"Stop!" Cat sighed and waved a dismissive hand. "Wait until I'm gone."

"Soon enough, I can call myself an ex-cop, if I like," Furbister said.

Cat shook her head as she and her bodyguards left the warehouse.

The two fake cops shared evil grins with each other as soon as Cat and her men were out the door.

"I call dibs on killing the dog and the chubby little broad," Mendlemann said.

"*She's* the one who knocked you out?" Furbister asked. "She may not even be five feet tall."

"Height aside," Mendlemann said, "she swings like Babe Ruth."

"Have it your way. I'll do the others. Just don't let that little broad take your gun this time." Furbister turned toward Al, Maury, and Fergie, and his eyes lit up in eagerness.

Suddenly, a rock the size of a golf ball bounced off Furbister's temple.

Fergie watched his eyes cross then go blank as he crumpled to the floor.

He'd just been reaching for his sidearm, and the gun fell to the concrete beside him in a clatter.

Mendlemann spun to look down at his fallen partner. He had his gun out and started to turn back toward the line of them when another rock the same size smacked him squarely in the forehead. His eyes started to cross, and his gun hand lowered.

Al rushed forward, dragging Fergie, Bonnie, and Tanner along with him. He kicked at the bending man, catching him in the stomach.

Fergie had a free leg, so she kicked at the side of Mendlemann's knee but got him in the low ribs instead. He started to crumple, then another rock hit him squarely on the temple, and he collapsed in a pile.

Bonnie was close enough to grab the Smith & Wesson pistol out of his hand before it could clatter to the warehouse floor. Al had all he could do to keep Tanner off the fallen men. Neither was stirring.

Fergie, like Al, was looking around in the direction from which the stones had come.

Out from behind one of the piles of tightly sealed crates rose the smiling face of Luke Boy. Beside him, Barky emerged as well. Both hustled toward them.

"Well, Abel Barkins," Al said. "I do owe you a big thank-you and an apology."

Barky grinned and held up a handcuff key. He went from one to the next, undoing their cuffs. Then he took the loose cuffs and put them on the ankles and wrists of the cops. "Them boys are gonna wake up with headaches for sure."

"That was some amazing slingshot shooting," Fergie told Luke Boy, whose wrist-rocket slingshot hung from his belt.

"He pesters the holy hell out of gulls, pelicans, and the occasional shark," Barky said. He turned and gave a loud whistle.

Big black Floy, of Floy's Place, came out from behind another stack of the crates. Without the apron, he looked even bigger, and he was giving a big, white-toothed grin as he came.

"What're you going to do about these men?" Al nodded to the cops on the floor. He was rubbing his wrists.

"Leave 'em here, I guess," Barky said. "Floy and I got some of the natives riled up enough to help if needed, but it's not in most of them to kill someone. That's the bailiwick of Catahoula Cathy but not us. In a real pinch, though, I guess we'll see."

"We're just making amends for not being squeaky wheels sooner," Floy said. "We all kinda hoped they'd pack up and move on sooner or later. I guess they needed more of a nudge."

"For now," Barky said, "let's say we get out of Dodge."

Holding a pistol in one hand, Bonnie handed the other sidearm to Al. He gave it to Fergie and busied himself with untying Tanner from his leg. He still had to hold the dog back from the fallen men. Tanner didn't bother Barky, Luke Boy, or Floy, so he must have had some sense of who were good guys and who weren't.

"Let's hope we don't need these guns," Al told Barky. "Fergie's a former Austin city detective, and Bonnie's the best shot of us. But both would have to go a ways to top the slingshot work of Luke Boy here."

The first mate grinned.

"You have the conn," Al told Barky. "Lead us out of here."

AT AL'S FIRST STEP outside the warehouse into the fresh, salty air of the outdoors, he took as deep a breath as he could and smiled at Fergie, who was doing the same. Even Tanner seemed to smile up at him. They rubbed their wrists and waited.

As soon as all the others were outside, Barky looked up and down the streets, saw no one that worried him, and waved them across the road. Then he led them down a block and around the corner, where a food truck sat waiting. Lettering on its side proclaimed Floy's Place. Al, Fergie, Tanner, Maury, Bonnie, Barky, and Luke Boy all climbed into the two doors open in the back. The smell of food, fried chicken in particular, swept over them, reminding them of how little they had eaten.

Al had once heard Maury tell Bonnie, "I'd sooner watch you walk than eat fried chicken." But as hungry as they were, he thought offering any of them a chicken leg right then would be a cruel test.

With no seats inside, they had to squat on the floor. While not packed in quite as tightly as sardines, they were cozy to a fault, with Tanner squirming around, trying to be on Al's lap first then on Fergie's. Maury had his arms around Bonnie, who was trying not to be giddy at having a chance of seeing her baby again. Neither Al nor Fergie wanted to say anything to dampen the moment, but they were far from free and clear yet. Floy barely glanced at them but took off the moment they were inside.

The streets seemed calmer since the cop cars had stopped searching for them. Once out on the main road, Floy drove west, in the direction of Port Aransas.

As he got closer to the edge of the city, he said, "Uh-oh."

Al rose enough to see the barricades and blue and red lights of a roadblock still up. Cars and trucks were lined up, waiting to be checked.

Floy turned off the main street, onto a side street going north.

Ah well. Al rubbed his wrists, petted Tanner, and put an arm around Fergie. They were free for the moment, and that felt huge. He wanted to savor that for as long as he could. They'd all believed they were just about to die, yet they were alive. Few feelings in life were better than that.

"Now where are we going?" Al asked.

"We think you probably need to meet a fella named Phil, and we just gotta get you off the streets," Floy said. "Well, all of us are probably gonna need to lie low once they find that those cops have done dropped the ball."

THE WAREHOUSE DOOR opened, and three of the Demon Dozen in their black combat gear stepped inside, carrying their cleaning supplies and body bags. As they started across the open warehouse floor, they tugged off their masks, as they wouldn't need them for the chore at hand.

"Well, shit on a biscuit," Max Varon said when he saw the two cops on the warehouse floor with their handcuffed wrists and ankles, squirming but with no chance of getting away.

Max yanked out his phone and punched in Cat's number.

"What?"

"They're loose again. All of them."

"And our little hired-hand cops?"

"Down and out."

"Doesn't that just restore my faith in Port Dexter's finest. I'll get everyone scrambling again on the hunt. The roadblocks are still up, but I'll get all hands on deck, looking for those miserable shitheads." She hesitated. "I think you know what we need to do. I'm pulling the plug. If we get this fixed pronto by some miracle, then we can get back in the saddle. Otherwise, it's plan B now and full speed ahead at that."

"Gotcha." Max hung up. "Get loading as many of those crates as you can into the vans," he told the other men. "I don't trust using the shrimper boats for that just now. You boys are about to make a road trip."

He went over to look down at the two cops in the center of the warehouse floor.

"Give us a hand here, Max," Furbister said.

"Yeah." Mendlemann's white bandage had some fresh red on it and had slipped down over one eye as he'd struggled.

"I expected to have to do some cleanup work here." Max stood over them. "What happened?"

"The villagers rose up," Furbister said. "That's what happened."

"You guys." Max shook his head and went down on one knee beside Furbister. "Aw, and they took your guns away from you, too, didn't they? What am I going to do with you?"

"Set us free. That's what." Furbister's voice was an angry snarl.

"Oh, I'll gladly do that for you," Max said. "Set you free. You see, this is one of them good-news-bad-news things for us. We already brought some body bags, and there's gonna be no blood to clean up."

He got a firm grip on Furbister's head and gave a sharp, hard twist that made a crack like a board being slapped against the concrete floor. Furbister's eyes snapped open wide, and he was staring as Max lowered the head to the floor. *Somewhere, a parole officer should be thanking me,* Max thought.

"What the hell?" Mendlemann struggled hard against the handcuffs. White rings showed in his wide-open eyes. "We're cops."

"You see, that's the thing," Max said. "You're not really cops. You're ex-con hired hands and not particularly good ones. You've failed again. And… you're expendable."

He reached down for Mendlemann's head.

The other two men didn't even look Max's way when another loud crack echoed off the warehouse walls.

Chapter Nineteen

As Max walked into the cupola, Cat was hanging up the phone she held. She barely glanced his way before looking back across the treetops toward the town—that troublesome damn town.

"That was the sheriff. This Jaime Avila is planning to arrive anyway, just him and a couple of his men," she said. "I said to try to stall him."

"And if that doesn't work?"

"Then discourage him... with prejudice."

He shrugged. "I've got men packing as much of the baled warehouse money as they can."

She nodded. "The sheriff is your concern right now. You'd better slip over that way and see if any help is needed."

As he left the room, she looked around. Though nothing new or different was there to see, she had the profound feeling that her house of cards was falling early.

"We're going to have to cut our losses and scramble," she said.

JAIME AVILA'S BLACK Hawk helicopter dropped onto the heliport pad adjacent to the main building of the sheriff's department complex on the outskirts of Port Dexter.

He'd been tempted to have Skippy, his pilot, pass over the town to see if he could spot anything out of the usual, but courtesy suggested he have his chat with the sheriff first.

His two men, Hank and Skippy, came along with him, all of them wearing their sidearms, Sig Sauer P320s, and their black short-sleeve uniform shirts with Police ICE in white block letters on the front. They left their vests in the copter. The visit was just a brief pop-in for information. He was planning to check in with the police department next.

Inside the brownish-red brick building, he was ushered down a short hallway into Sheriff Sanderson's office.

Sanderson looked young for a sheriff, maybe in his forties. He had a full head of dark hair with a bit of a hat-hair ring around it. The hat, with its golden-braid hatband, was hanging on a wall peg.

He pushed aside a file and stood to shake hands, giving a little more to the squeeze than was needed. "What brings you down to these parts? Planning to sneak in a little fishing?"

"No fishing. I got a text from a friend saying I should come check out the town."

"Maybe you'd best ask the friend what he meant. It's business as usual for us. Hardly a ripple in the pond. The occasional drunk or domestic quarrel but nothing exciting like you guys enjoy." He shook his head. "Just where is this friend of yours?"

"I'm not sure. I haven't been able to reach him again."

"Is this the sort of friend who might play a prank?"

"No. He usually says what he means and means what he says."

"Good for him—a rare kind of man these days. But I don't know what he might have meant. We're calm to the point of being pathetic around here."

Jaime had noticed the glass door to the dispatcher's room was closed, so he couldn't hear anything. But the place seemed to have a suppressed bustle about it.

The sheriff got a call on his cell phone. He held up an apologetic finger to request a moment. He stepped away to listen, then he said, "I understand," and hung up.

Jaime thought the sheriff's eyes had narrowed a bit.

"Well, if you don't mind, I'll take a quick look around town," Jaime said.

"Fine with me. But you'll be wasting your time."

The sheriff stood up but didn't offer the usual dismissive hand-shake.

Jaime and his men went back to the hallway then out through the front door. He sensed everyone was paying far too much attention to them as they passed.

The breeze swept across him as they walked toward the helipad, but that wasn't what sent the cool chill of a shadow brushing across his spine.

He glanced back. A group of half a dozen deputies was pouring out the front door, each holding a long gun. The sheriff was at their front, a pistol in his hand.

A roar of an engine just over a low hill grew as a black Sikorsky S-76 helicopter rose, and a door gunner fired a rocket launcher that blew up Jaime's Black Hawk.

"Get down!" Jaime yelled. "And I don't mean dance!"

He spun as his men dove to hug the ground. Sheriff Sanderson had slipped on a bulletproof vest like the others. *So it's all going rock and roll here.*

A couple of deputies stopped running to open fire.

Jaime stood his ground long enough to sight a careful shot right to the sheriff's head. The sheriff fell to the ground in a pile of loose arms and legs.

That slowed the deputies for only half a minute.

Jaime joined his men on the grass, crawling toward a depression in the ground, their only hope of cover. He tugged out his cell phone as he went and called his office.

"We've got a situation here. Send a Special Response Team. Hell, send two of them."

The SRTs were ICE's elite tactical squads, the equivalent of a SWAT team.

He put his phone away, knowing that even if they came as soon as they could, that would probably be too late. Calling the local police would likely be a waste of time as well.

Two of the deputies coming at him fell to the ground as he and his men returned fire. But they were pinned down and outnumbered.

The S-76 helicopter lowered to the ground, and four men poured out and ran in Jaime's direction.

His phone rang. He didn't recognize the number but answered, hoping for someone from his office.

"It's me, Al Quinn."

"Got another phone?" Jaime asked.

"Yeah, this one's Floy's. Where are you?"

"I just got to town. What the hell did you call about in the first place?"

"Human trafficking, money laundering, massive grand theft auto, murder, and underage prostitution, to name a few. A woman named Catahoula Cathy Castleton is the kingpin behind it all. I can give you her address. She has a mercenary mini army. They dress in black. Could be Goth."

"I know about the sheriff's department by now, but what about the police?"

"Both bent and under her thumb."

"I wish you'd told me that sooner. I've got deputies shooting at me right now, and my copter just got blown up. Their copter has just landed, and I've got what are probably the mercenaries you mentioned coming my way from the other direction. We're pinned down here."

"Can't rescue us? Okay. I'll come out your way and try to rescue you."

"Just get here pronto, before my two men and I run out of ammo."

"Okay. I'm on it."

"Let me emphasize again the pronto, eh, old buddy?"

AL HANDED FLOY'S PHONE back to him. "Okay. We've got to hurry. Shots are being fired right now. Who can get us to the sheriff's department as fast as possible?"

They were hiding in the pawn shop of a man named Phil Rosenbeirn.

"My food truck's about the only thing that can hold several of you," Floy said.

"I can pile in, too, and promise I won't take up too much room," Phil said. He was an extremely skinny man who'd looked young at first until Al got a closer look at the man's hair, almost stiff with black dye. The man's eyes bugged out so that with the hair and his build, he looked like a Mr. Bean gone emo. But he was having a real hoot of a time consorting with Al, Fergie, Bonnie, and Maury, who had all picked out guns from his stock.

As soon as they'd arrived at Phil's store a while back, he'd let them pick from some of his most expensive stock of weapons.

Floy's eyes had popped. "I gotta tell you folks that Phil here is usually an extremely parsimonious man. There was a time you couldn't get a nickel out of his fist with the jaws of life. He's giving you the good stuff, even though he knows he might never see a dime for it."

Al had the police .38 he'd gotten at the warehouse and also picked out a .357 Colt Python with a six-inch barrel. He'd offered it to Fergie, but it had been a little heavy in her hand. She had opted for a well-worn .380 Glock 42. Phil had ammo for them.

Barky and Luke Boy looked on but didn't pick out any weapons. Al wasn't sure what kind of real help they would be once any fireworks started. But at least they were stirring up other locals and helping to some extent.

"Having the police department switched out on us at the first threw us," Phil said. "It was like our world went upside down."

"Isn't the sheriff an elected official?" Fergie asked Phil. "How did he come to be playing for the opposition?"

"Well, the thing about Harlan Sanderson is that he was a good guy when he was elected, had experience as a trusted deputy, and had a good, clean record."

"But it turned out," Floy said, "that he also had a price tag."

"He could be bought?" Maury asked.

"Quickly and easily." Phil went over to the cash register and drew a Samuel Walker single-action Colt .44 from beneath it. "This is my deterrent to discourage shoplifters. It's loaded, and folks know I have it." The gun looked almost too heavy and cumbersome for his sticklike build. "Don't you worry. I've had it out on the range and learned to ride its buck. It does have quite a kick."

Next he took down a double-barrel Stoeger coach gun and handed it to Floy. "If they get close, this might keep you alive. It's only six and a half pounds, and the twenty-inch barrels make it legal." He broke open the back and popped in a couple of shells. "It's easy for anyone to use." He slid the rest of the box of shells toward Floy.

Barky shook his head when offered a gun, as did Luke Boy, but the first mate did have his slingshot.

"Oh, we're one fine army now," Floy said.

Though a bit lost without her usual peashooter, the .38 Chiefs Special, Bonnie did have the police Smith & Wesson .38 in her belt and picked out a .30-06 with a scope. She picked up a box of ammo for both.

"She's the best shot of us," Fergie told Phil. "He's the worst shot." She nodded toward Maury, who held a Remington V3 tactical twelve-gauge shotgun, which Phil had said kicked very little.

"People sure pawn their guns a lot," Maury said, looking at the rack of long guns and the case of pistols.

"Guitars too." Phil waved at the far wall, which was filled with electric and acoustic guitars, mandolins, and a fiddle or two.

"Let's go," Al said. "We've really got to roll."

They quickly crowded into the back of Floy's food truck and sat on the floor—Al, Maury, Bonnie, Fergie, Tanner, Barky, and Luke Boy—while the cook fired up the engine and took off at a pretty good pace. Phil sat up front beside Floy. Those crowded into the small space in the back had no room to even fidget as the truck rumbled along at what was probably its best speed possible.

Tanner was sniffing at a small fridge behind Al.

"They's some sausages in there that're cooked and mighty tasty if you're the least bit peckish." Floy kept his eyes on the road and took a turn sharp enough that they were all thrown to one side, piling atop one another, Tanner included.

Once righted, they pulled themselves apart. A bungee cord held the fridge door closed. Al took that off long enough to pull out a handful of dark smoked sausages. He handed each of them one and was going to split his with Tanner, who grabbed the one Al held and went off to a corner to lower himself to chew away. Al got another sausage out for himself and sealed the door again.

He felt as though they hadn't eaten anything in forever.

Bonnie found a case of water bottles wrapped in clear plastic. She tore a hole at one end and handed a bottle to each of them.

They ate like animals, including Tanner. Al had Fergie pour some water into his cupped hands so that Tanner could lap some up.

Al had been on many trips like that years ago back in his military days—no one talked about where they were going or what they intended to do, just riding along and keeping their minds occupied with almost anything else until the doors opened and they had to charge out.

The ride took only seven minutes. They could hear gunfire as Floy slid the truck to a stop in some gravel.

Though their ride had been snug to a fault, none of the folks after them in town could have expected a food truck to be their getaway vehicle, nor could they have foreseen the lot of them tumbling out the back doors like clowns from a circus car.

"Let's go, boys and girls." Al handed the end of Tanner's leash to Barky as he rushed out the door. "We've got to hit them with a charge."

As though they'd done that sort of thing many times before, the others spread out to either side of him as they hurried forward as fast as they could toward the fury of shots being fired.

"You guys stay back and protect the food truck!" Al yelled back to Barky.

He and Luke Boy were still standing beside it, showing no eagerness to join the fray of those with all the guns. Al hoped Floy and Phil would stay back too.

Al ran as quickly as he could. Fergie was always faster on the run, and she was out in front.

Bonnie stood on a small grass-covered mound to one side of them and had the scope of her rifle up to her eye. She began to fire away, laying down an effective cover.

Two deputies fell, one after the other, like ducks at a shooting gallery. The rest of the deputies dove to the ground or fell back, scrambling to get out of range. One fell even while on the run. Another of Bonnie's bullets had found a home.

One of the men in black, who'd gotten up to run, suddenly tumbled to the ground. Bonnie's shot had hit home again. Her rifle swung back toward the deputies.

Fergie suddenly rushed to her left, with Maury, Floy, and Phil right behind her. *So much for keeping most of them at the truck.* At least Barky and Luke Boy were back there, with Tanner to protect them.

A flurry of shotgun blasts came from out of sight to Al's left then the big boom of Phil's Colt.

After a minute, Fergie led the way back to close ranks with Al. "They were trying to flank us from that direction!" she yelled.

One of the men in black stood to fire steady shots their way. A shot from Bonnie's rifle sent the gun flying out of his hands. A second shot rocked his head back, and he crumpled.

The remaining two men in black took off running back toward their copter.

Bonnie hit one of them on the run, not an easy feat when shooting with a scoped rifle. He dropped his gun and was limping as the other helped him into the copter and closed the door.

The copter rose into the air and turned toward them. Bonnie raised her gun and fired. She worked the bolt and fired again. A hole the size of a tennis ball appeared in its windshield, then another bullet thumped into its metal side near its auxiliary fuel tank.

That was enough for the pilot. He spun the copter and headed away, probably not as fast as he could go, which was over one hundred seventy miles per hour, but he was getting out of range as quickly as possible with a damaged windshield. The S-76 was more suited to commercial use and lacked the armor of a combat helicopter.

A couple of the remaining deputies were trying to help a wounded deputy to his feet, while others formed into a knot and charged toward Jaime and his men. Before they could get to them, Floy and Phil had taken off again, running from the right and opening fire. Phil's Sam Walker Colt boomed with each shot, and Floy's double-barrel stagecoach shotgun roared even louder as he fired both barrels. He had the gun open and was shoving in two more shells as he ran, perhaps faster than he'd sprinted since his days on the gridiron.

The deputies who could move quickly did so as they turned and ran in the other direction, leaving one or two wounded behind.

By the time Al and the others got to where Jaime and his two men had hunkered down, all the opposing sheriff's deputies had retreated all the way inside their building. The sheriff still lay on the ground along with three of his deputies that Al could see. Maybe more were over the hill where some had been caught trying to sneak around.

"Give me a hand with this man," Jaime said.

Al turned around and saw two men already bent over one of Jaime's companions, who'd been hit in the shoulder. Out of nowhere, Barky and Luke Boy had rushed forward to help. Tanner, on the end of the leash Barky held, was growling at the deputies who'd been firing at them. Luke Boy had yanked off his T-shirt, and Barky was tearing it into strips and packing the cloth around the entry and exit wounds.

Floy and Phil moved close to stand over them, holding their weapons ready.

"Easy with Skippy," Jaime said. "He's the pilot."

"With nothing to fly." Skippy rose high enough to look at the black smoke rolling upward from what used to be a heavily armed helicopter. "I could have taken them if we'd been in the air."

One of the nearest wounded deputies propped himself up and started to raise his gun toward them. Before either Floy or Phil could lift a weapon, Luke Boy spun, pulled his slingshot out of his belt, and sent a rock flying to hit the deputy in the head. The gun fell from the deputy's hand as he dropped back to the ground.

"It's kinda fun now that I know they're bad guys," Luke Boy said. He turned back to helping Barky.

Barky and Luke Boy carefully lifted Skippy onto his feet. Then they took off, hurrying the pilot over to the food truck, not knowing how much time they would have. Floy and Phil went along behind to provide cover. Jaime went over to have a quick look at the two downed men in black. He bent to yank off their skull masks. "Should have known. These two guys have sold their souls to cartels or anyone willing to hire them. Give me a hand getting their gear, Hank."

The other ICE agent came over, took off the gun belt, and picked up the AR-15.

"I'm feeling better about this now," Jaime said as he carried the belt and semiautomatic rifle away.

As Jaime joined the others heading for the truck, he spotted Bonnie, who'd put two of the pistols from the fallen deputies under her belt, and she was carrying the .30-06.

"I should have known," Jaime said. "That was some real Annie Oakley shooting there."

"I only wish I was as good with a slingshot as that Luke Boy," she said.

"Good to see you, too, Fergie, and you, Maury." Jaime glanced at the others.

"It's like old home week," Maury said.

"And I don't know where you rounded up these other guys"—Jaime waved a hand toward Barky, Luke Boy, Floy, and Phil—"but they were sure parachutes coming out of the sky."

"We didn't round them up," Al said. "They rounded us up and saved us as well. They represent the local contingent."

"We'd better get a wiggle on," Fergie said.

"Are there many more of them?" Jaime asked.

"Lots," Al said. "Way more than I'd like."

"Then let's get the hell out of here," Jaime said.

Barky was still holding Tanner's leash. They all ran toward the truck. Luke Boy was grinning like someone watching the home team coming off the field after a football game.

They all scrambled into the back of the truck, even though more people had to squeeze inside. Barky and Luke Boy stretched out Jaime's pilot, Skippy, on the floor, making the others press back to give him room. Bonnie and Fergie hovered closest over him and were tearing towels, wetting them from a bottle of water, and dabbing at the man's wound. Floy fired up his truck, put it in gear, and took off.

"I don't know when I've been as glad to see you," Jaime said to Al. "I've called for backup, but this was far bigger than I expected."

"We've had some communication issues," Al said, "or I would've let you know all about this sooner. I don't even know if this is something for your group."

"It is now." Jaime was looking down at Skippy.

"We've got two sheriff's cruisers lighting up behind us," Floy called to those in the back.

"As you can see," Al said, "we're far from being out of the woods yet."

Chapter Twenty

"There's no way you can outrun those guys behind us, Floy." Al tilted his head toward the sound of the approaching sirens.

"It's kind of hard to disguise a food truck, too, one with my name on the side of it," the man said. "They probably have my plate number too."

"If they were real deputies, you might have an issue," Fergie said. "By now, we've figured out that the only real lawman was the sheriff himself, and he'd sold himself to the highest bidder."

"I'm starting to feel better about having shot that sheriff," Jaime said.

"The worst was that he was one of us," Phil said. "We voted the tomfool into office. Who knew his eyes would light up with dollar signs?"

Jaime rose, wriggled through the crowded truck, and looked out the back window at the two cruisers with lights and sirens going. "Al's right. You're not going to be able to outrun them, Floy."

"I hear you on that."

"Pull over and stop. Hank, get ready."

Jaime pressed close to the door. He and Hank checked the selection switches on the AR-15s they held.

Floy veered onto the right shoulder, where he stopped abruptly. Jaime flung the back door open.

He and Hank were out in a flash, and each dropped to a firing stance on one knee. They aimed for the tires of the cruisers coming directly toward them.

They took out the front tires of the lead car in a flurry of shots. Its front end fell to the asphalt, scraping along on rims throwing sparks. With a jerk, it spun off the road to its right.

Jaime and Hank kept firing. The second car's driver was already slamming on his brakes, trying to avoid their barrage. That cruiser was skidding as both its front tires blew, and it came to a grinding stop.

Jaime and Hank hopped back into the truck and slammed the rear doors shut.

Floy was already throwing gravel as he peeled out, getting back onto the road.

"That should buy us a little time," Jaime said.

"Until we get to the city cops," Fergie said, "and whatever remaining creepy Goth guys this Cat woman has left."

Because of the wounded man in the back, Floy headed toward the hospital. But he'd only gone a mile or two before red and blue lights flickered ahead as police cars chased back and forth.

"The ol' truck was a good cover earlier," Floy said, "but I'm starting to feel conspicuous driving around now that it's turned into a bull's-eye."

"I think Skippy can wait if we can get him somewhere quiet and doctor him a bit ourselves," Jaime replied.

"I have an idea," Al said. "There might be a place where we could lie low and hide out until Jaime's backup can get here."

"I think I know exactly where you have in mind," Bonnie said. "There's only one sure place you can go where no one would think of looking. You're going to head right into the lion's den, aren't you?"

Fergie shook her head. "Oh no."

"It's our best chance."

"You don't have to sell me," Fergie said, "but I think Skippy could still use some professional medical attention. He's lost a bit of blood."

"That's not an option. We've got to try it," Al said. "Maybe we can get our hands on some Band-Aids there."

MAX VARON CAME INTO the bedroom and caught Catahoula Cathy throwing underwear and dresses into a Louis Vuitton suitcase.

"Ah, I didn't know you wore underwear," he said. He was wearing his combat gear but had his mask off.

"And you were never going to find out," she said. When he didn't say anything, she looked up. "How bad is it out there?"

"I'd say the tide is turning."

"In numbers!" she yelled.

"We've lost the sheriff and, by now, probably most of his department. There have been a few losses among the police too."

He didn't mention the bodies of Furbister and Mendlemann, which he'd dumped into the gulf. Their clothes had gone into a fire with the rest of the cleanup materials.

"I have six men left, counting myself and the two driving the SUVs with the money. They should be out of town by now. The windshield is busted on the Sikorsky S-76. We had to leave it at the little local airport. A guy can't get out to work on it until next week, no matter what we offered him."

"Good help is so hard to find these days," she muttered.

"You're telling me."

She stopped what she was doing and looked up at him. "If push comes to shove, will you still stand by me?"

"You know the answer to that. I do what I'm paid to do."

"That's what I thought." She went over to the dresser and opened a matching Louis Vuitton briefcase. It was completely filled with bundled stacks of one-hundred-dollar Federal Reserve notes. Each bundle was worth ten thousand dollars. She grabbed a couple of bundles and tossed them to Max.

He caught them and lifted them to smell them. He riffled the end of one.

"Will that get us through the afternoon?" she asked.

"It's a start."

AL DIDN'T NEED TO GIVE Floy directions once they mentioned the estate where Cat had been staying.

"Hell, I even catered there a couple of times for the previous residents," Floy said. "It was the winter place for some folks from Maine. But their family line died out not too long ago, and the place sat empty for a spell." Floy drove past the closed front gate of Cat's place.

When he slowed, Fergie said, "If you're thinking of pulling over into that blind lane to the left, don't. They found us there once."

He turned around a mile down the road at a place with enough room to get his truck headed in the other direction. They were coming around a stand of woods at a bend in the road when he slowed to a stop and started to back up, keeping his eye on the rearview mirror.

"What?" Jaime stood and tried to peer ahead.

"The gate was opening," Floy said. "Someone get out and keep an eye on it."

Phil already had the back door open and was outside. Jaime scrambled right behind him. The two went out of sight around a bend, where Al knew they could stay in the trees but still see Cat's front gate.

Barely two minutes later, they came running back to the food truck to climb back inside.

"You can go, Floy," Jaime said. "A black SUV just headed out the gate, and I think they left it open. I'm betting the rats are leaving the sinking ship."

Floy drove up until he was just outside the gate. No traffic seemed to be coming from either direction.

Phil hopped out the back, approached the gate, and shot inside. He was gone less than five minutes. When he returned, he climbed into the back and said, "Looks okay to me. Not a soul in sight."

Floy turned in through the gate.

"Gonna drive right up to the front door, eh?" Hank asked.

"Fortune favors the bold," Floy said.

"I like these guys," Jaime said. "I still don't know how you connected, but I like them."

Al decided not to tell Jaime that Floy was a fry cook in his daytime gig, but perhaps Jaime had already figured that out, since Floy's name was on the food truck.

"Before we move him inside"—Jaime waved a hand at Skippy—"we'd better sweep this place and make sure it's emptied out all the way and no one is lurking inside."

Bonnie, the former nurse, stayed with Skippy as well as Barky and Luke Boy.

Al, Fergie, Maury, Hank, Floy, Phil, and Jaime all checked their weapons and headed toward the house. Jaime signaled Hank and Phil to join him in going around to check the four-car garage and the back of the house.

They eased up to the front of the two-story building, keeping an eye on the windows and the grounds to either side. No one popped up to give them a hard time.

Al reached for the front door. It was locked. He turned to Maury, who grinned. From his left front pocket he took out a worn brown leather folder that opened to show a row of picks, each in its own leather sheath.

"Got it at Phil's store. When my eyes lit up, he said I could have it." Maury selected two picks and bent close to the lock, fiddling away, the tip of his tongue out the side of his mouth. In under a minute, he stood and said, "Voilà."

Al twisted the knob, and the door opened. He and Fergie rushed through and covered the room with their pistols. The high-ceiling foyer was empty—just bare wooden floors and not a stick of furniture, not even drapes or blinds on the windows. The hallway ahead was as empty. Two sweeping stairways went left and right up to the next floor. The place was so hollow that Al could practically hear the beat of his heart echoing.

He gave the all-clear sign to Floy and Maury. Once they were inside, Al pointed toward the staircases. Floy and Maury, each with a shotgun, started upward, one to each side.

Al and Fergie started checking the downstairs rooms, one by one.

What struck Al right away was that most of the rooms downstairs were empty except for two to four cots—twelve cots in all. The one bathroom and half bath on the floor must have done for everyone staying on that floor.

The kitchen was almost as bare and sad as the rest. An almost empty crate of MREs—military-style meals ready to eat—sat on one counter with an empty crate of tuna cans. The fridge held only bottles of water. The tenants had sure lived a Spartan existence.

After opening the back door to let in Jaime, Hank, and Phil, Al shook his head.

All four of them went upstairs to the next floor. Almost every room there was empty as well, as if the house was being prepped to show to prospective buyers.

Only the master bedroom and bath on that floor looked lived in at all. A mini fridge in that room held carbonated water and half a package of oatmeal breakfast bars.

Up in the cupola, a solitary metal folding chair sat pointed in the direction of Port Dexter.

The whole house had been only temporary quarters while they milked the town for all they could get out of it.

Imagine, Al thought, *someone raking in that kind of money and living as if in poverty.* That was a life obsessively about money and only money. *Did she plan to buy luxuries at some later day, or was just getting it all that mattered?*

"You can practically hear yourself echo in this big, hollow house," Fergie said. "She even told us she had a staff hairdresser living with her, but there's no sign of one. Why would she lie about a thing like that? It's really more pitiful than anything, to have the kind of money she had to be raking in and deny herself almost every amenity."

They all headed back to the kitchen. Jaime was on his cell phone the whole time.

"My backup is still forty minutes to an hour away." Jaime lowered his phone then lifted it again. "I've got a couple more calls to make, one to the Gulf Coast Violent Offenders Task Force. Since human trafficking was involved here, I've got another call to make to Danielle Cassidy, who still heads up that group out of the Houston FBI office."

They set up a cot with clean sheets and carried Skippy in to put him in the room nearest the kitchen.

Barky moved closer to the cot. "Were you in the navy once?"

"Yep." Skippy grinned.

"I was too," Barky said. "Welcome aboard."

"You see any action?"

"Way too much. It's the quiet life of shrimping for me now. I do like being on the water."

"I flew copters and got to be on the water," Skippy said, "so win-win."

Fergie came back into the room and held out a first-aid kit she'd found upstairs. Bonnie grabbed it while Barky and Luke Boy went to the kitchen to get her a bucket or a pan of water and anything she could use as bandages. Both had plenty of experience patching each other up in the occasional accidents that happened in a career on the water.

Floy headed outside to move his truck around and park it in the oversize garage, since the doorways were high enough to accommodate an RV.

Bonnie's movements were skillful and brisk, the result of years of experience as a nurse. She carefully washed out Skippy's entrance and exit wounds, dabbed in some Neosporin she got from a little tube, because that was all she had, put gauze over the wounds, and tore off strips of zinc oxide tape with her teeth to hold the gauze in place.

She stood up. "That should hold him. He needs rest. We have no way of giving him any blood, but some broth wouldn't hurt."

Skippy's eyes were closed, as he was either asleep or just resting. Barky looked like he wanted to pat his fellow Navy veteran on the other shoulder, but he held back.

Fergie leaned close to Al and echoed his earlier notion. "Living like this showed extreme focus to an objective, but it was a damned lonely way to be," she said, "and would sting worse if things ever went horribly wrong, as I hope they do."

"When we get home, let's savor life more and go off our diets now and then. Live!" he said. "That is, if we get home."

"*When* we get home. Let's make that *when* we get home."

Chapter Twenty-One

Cat was in a mood, a funk that would have signaled a migraine if she were prone to them. She didn't look out the vehicle's windows at any of Port Dexter's small houses or the first few businesses on the upper end of the town they drove past.

"I have some bad news for you," Max said. He'd driven twenty miles above the speed limit most of the way toward downtown Port Dexter.

"Can it wait?" Cat had tilted her seat back and was staring at the roof.

The two other remaining members of her Demon Dozen sat quietly, one in the front and the other beside her. They were wearing their masks and full combat gear, like Max, except his mask was off while he drove. The wounded one had patched himself up and said he was good to go. He'd been moving around with barely a limp.

"I think you should know," Max said.

She sighed. "Well, let me have it."

"The two SUVs we had heading off to the east—"

"The ones with almost all the money?"

"They've just been stopped." He pointed at the earpiece in his right ear. "They say they're surrounded by six FBI vans and what looks like a full tactical squad. Oh, and two copters are overhead. Seems the feds were on the lookout for black SUVs, like this one, moving in tandem. They're outnumbered ten to one and outgunned by more than that, so they're not gonna try to fight it out. They're getting out of the vehicles."

"Quitters," Cat said. "Cowards."

Max paused then reached up to tug out the earpiece and put it on the console. "Well, that's that."

"All that money," Cat said. "All that sweet, sweet money. Those bastards did this to us, those meddlesome jackasses who came nosing around. They should have been fish chum by now, twice over. Why, oh why, do bad things happen to me?"

"Well, crap." Max glanced back. "You'd better hold on to that thought. Things are about to get worse."

Cat sat up. "What now?"

"Look at this mess up ahead."

Cat could see flashing lights, but the police didn't look like the ones she had in her pocket. Some new folks had come to town, real cops and probably more of those blasted federal ones at that. Black SUVs and larger SWAT vans were parked in rings around the nearest bar and motel within sight, and the others were probably just as swarmed. *Yeah, it's federal.*

How in the world did all this happen and so quickly? She'd started out that morning with three bulletproof Cadillac Escalades, that year's model, a helicopter, and enough money to buy an island or at least to go somewhere else to live well and lie low. All that had come crashing down. Her insides were boiling.

"We can't go forward into that." Max turned onto a side street.

Other cars were scurrying away from the doings downtown, perhaps visitors to the bars and motels who'd gotten away just in time or even some of the fake police who'd shucked their uniforms and were heading for the hills.

Max steered into the flow of them as they were all swept along in one direction like citizens evacuating in the face of a coming hurricane.

It was a hurricane, all right, and one she had to flee as well.

"Oh yeah." Max was glancing at the screen of a cell phone on the dash. "Here's one more bit of a news flash for you. Someone has breached the defenses back at the house. The alarm is sounding."

"There's nothing in there worth saving."

"But I can only think of one bunch of people stupid and eager enough to come swarming into the place where we stayed."

"Do you think we could or should give them a horrible surprise?"

"If so, I think we can kill two birds with one stone—revenge and elimination at last," Max said. "The alarm system says they're still inside the house."

"Can you see them?"

"All the cameras are covering the outside and the grounds."

"Then let's give them a wake-up call. Have you got anything really big with you?"

Max nodded and drove faster until the driveway was just ahead.

Cat sat up straighter as the SUV turned in through the open gate and headed up the drive to pull up facing the front of the building. One corner of her mouth twitched up as eagerness swept through her. *Those blasted pests.*

Max got out and went around to the back of the SUV. On top of a pile of AR-15s, one rocket launcher was left. He carried it to the front of their vehicle to face the house, while Cat and the other two mercenaries stood to one side, aiming their AR-15s.

"Are you sure?" Max asked.

"It's a rental," Cat said. "Screw the deposit. Fire away when you're ready."

Max lifted the rocket launcher, aimed just above the front door, and pulled the trigger.

FERGIE LOOKED OVER the scruffy lot of them, herself included. They were tired, hungry, and worn to a frazzle. Each looked like they'd crawled out of the woods after a sleepless night.

All of them—Al, Fergie, Maury, Bonnie, Jaime, Hank, Barky, Luke Boy, Floy, and Phil—were gathered in an empty room, away from Skippy's cot, where he seemed to be asleep.

Bonnie borrowed Jaime's phone and called the motel. She got Mary Doughrety on the second ring. She talked only a minute, hung up, and handed the phone back to Jaime. "She says Little Al and Patty Belle are both just fine and that she has kept her lips zipped and hasn't said a word to you-know-who. She admitted she started to waver once for half a moment, but when she turned, there was Patty Belle standing between her and the phone, glaring and waving one finger back and forth. She said, 'That little gal is as sharp as a tack, no matter how she looks,' a kind of backhanded compliment. But I'm glad Patty Belle is on the case there."

Though that should've cheered her, she looked far from cheerful as she went to take a quick peek at how Skippy's wounds were doing. Maury caught enough in her expression to go put an arm around Bonnie.

Floy pulled out his own phone. "I'll see if I can rustle up some more local support as we free ourselves from the chains of this recent crime oppression."

"The more, the merrier." Jaime replied.

"Is anyone else hungry?" Phil asked.

Most of them nodded.

Floy finished calling a dozen people he thought could help form some grassroots resistance. He put away his phone.

Fergie smiled. Being connected to the world again, being able to communicate, sure was nice.

"Hey, Floy," Phil said, "there's hardly anything worth eating in the kitchen here. What do you say to rustling up some food for us in your truck?"

"Okay with me." Floy patted his stomach. "I'm a bit peckish myself."

"You guys go ahead. I'm not hungry," Bonnie said.

"Really?" Fergie asked. "This from the woman who once said she could eat the butt off a skunk?"

"She's hungry and needs to eat." Maury hugged Bonnie and told her, "You need to keep up your strength. Think of Little Al. We'll be seeing him soon, and he won't recognize you if you're whittled down to the stick figure Fergie has."

"Hey!" Fergie said.

"I can stay and see to Skippy while you're gone," Hank said. "That's what teammates do. But I'd be okay if you bring me back something to eat."

"And maybe Floy can whip up some broth for Skippy," Bonnie said. "As soon as he can, he needs to take in a little something. I'd better come along. I could maybe eat a burger or a pizza or two pizzas or two burgers and a pizza."

"Consider your orders placed," Floy said. "C'mon, the rest of you." He waved a hand and started toward the garage, where they'd parked his food truck.

They left their long guns in the room with Hank and Skippy, carrying just their sidearms as they headed off.

As they went, Bonnie was talking, not to Maury but to the imaginary Little Al in her head. "I'll be there as soon as we get shed of this hellhole."

"Hey!" Floy said. "This town's no hellhole."

"Well, it is for now," she said.

"You gotta give it to her," Phil said. "We're out here doing what we're doing because the town we grew up in needed a hard shake-up. And we're just the guys to do that."

Floy had hooked up the food truck to a power outlet when he'd parked, so he had only to open up and go inside. "Give me a minute while I fire up the deep fryer. Then I can do shrimp baskets, hush puppies, fries, fried okra, or about just about anything else tasty you can imagine. Meanwhile, I can be grilling up burgers, sausages, fried bologna, or grilled cheese sandwiches."

Even though she normally avoided those kinds of food, Fergie watched Floy cook with fascination.

He moved briskly, with the efficiency of someone used to having many people waiting but still wanting to give them the best meal possible.

Also, something was enormously comforting and human about the smell of food being cooked. They stood outside his window like customers, and he handed out dishes as quickly as they were ready.

Fergie and Al got a shrimp basket to share with each other and with Tanner, who ate one of the tails that fell to the ground and was rewarded with the rest of the tails and a whole shrimp or two. She let Al have all the fries, although Jaime and Phil helped themselves to some of those while they waited their turns.

Jaime reached for a basket of blackened catfish and deep-fried okra and asked, "Can you whip up something for my two men? Maybe soup for Skippy or some broth like Bonnie said, and whatever you've got for Hank."

As he spoke, an explosion rocked the front of the house.

He slid his basket back onto the food truck's counter and took off at a run.

Chapter Twenty-Two

Cat watched Max slip another rocket into the launcher with prac-
ticed ease. He lifted it and fired again.

The whole front of the house collapsed. She could see all the way to
the middle of the house once the huge cloud of dust and smoke cleared.
What was left of the walls looked like the ribs of a skeleton. That made
her grin.

The other two of Max's men stood on either side of him and swept
the gaping insides, firing at anything they thought they saw moving.

From around the back of the house, a group of people came running in their direction.

"Blast it! They weren't all inside," Cat said.

Max put down the rocket launcher and picked up his AR-15. The
other two had already begun to fire on the group, who hit the dirt at
the first shots going their way.

Some of those on the ground had handguns and were firing back,
so Cat slipped around to the other side of the bulletproof SUV. The element of surprise she thought they'd had was gone. But her men seemed
to have more firepower.

"Go get them! Finish them off. All of them!" Cat yelled.

Her men, the remaining three of her Demon Dozen, advanced
steadily, laying down a steady barrage of rifle fire, pulling clips from
their belts, reloading, and firing more with each step.

AS SOON AS AL AND THE others rounded the corner of the house, they saw three of the mercenaries in black shooting into the guts of the ruined house. They wore their masks but could see well enough to swing their guns toward Al and the others and fire away.

Even as the barrels were moving toward them, Al knocked Maury and Barky flat to the ground. Fergie did the same for Floy and Luke Boy, though all she had to do for Floy was to trip him and let momentum do the rest. Phil and Jaime both had enough battles in their backgrounds to already be on the ground. Wanting to charge, Tanner surged against his leash, which Barky held. Al helped press the overeager dog low to the ground.

For a few moments, it looked to Al like the mercenaries were going to stand there and shoot away, the way men did battle during the Revolutionary War. That Cat woman, though, had slipped around behind the black SUV at the first sound of a shot being fired at them.

Then her men moved forward steadily until a rock thunked one of them in the face. He yanked his mask off and reached up to a lump already starting to swell above his right eye.

Good for you, Luke Boy, Al thought. *Good for you.*

"Are you all right, Max?" the woman called out.

"No, I'm not bloody all right."

He and the other men in black pulled back to crouch or lie flat by the SUV.

The shooting on both sides picked up, although Al knew how limited the ammo was on his side. They'd left most of it inside with their long guns in Skippy's room.

"How're you doing on ammo?" Al called out.

"About out!" Bonnie yelled.

Even Luke Boy seemed to have run out of rocks for his slingshot. For a spell, Al had been hearing steady thuds as rocks slammed into the black SUV.

Al crawled to Bonnie and gave her half the .38 bullets he had in the pockets of his jeans. "Make every one of these bullets count."

She nodded, already shoving ammo into the gun she held.

MAURY HAD NOWHERE NEAR the experience of Al, Fergie, or even Bonnie with life-or-death shootouts, especially one of such intensity. Bullets were whizzing past, inches above his head, and he had no gun as the others did. He clung to the grass in the dip in the lawn that partially sheltered them.

He glanced over at Barky and Luke Boy. They were in much the same situation, except for Luke Boy popping up to work his magic with his slingshot. But even he was reaching around on the ground but finding nothing he could use for ammo.

Barky had his hands full keeping Tanner from standing and charging the men shooting at them. The dog would surely be shot in seconds if he had his way, but that didn't mean he didn't pull and push against Barky's grip while the man tried to keep him pressed to the ground.

Tanner made a sudden burst and nearly got free of Barky's grasp. Maury scurried closer, keeping as low as he could, and reached to help keep Tanner pressed to the ground. He felt a sting on the arm holding Tanner down and pressed harder so that he and the dog were just beneath the steady hail of bullets coming their way.

Blood welled up on his arm and oozed into a dripping line. None of the others seemed to have been hit, but that would all change when they ran out of ammo and those bastards in black charged them with fresh clips in their guns.

He wished Bonnie wouldn't rise and shoot as often as she did, but when she caught him watching her, she winked. At least something was taking her mind off being away from her little baby for the first time.

Maury tried to imagine them all at home again, peaceful and happy. But in the steady booming of shots exchanged, he couldn't seem to think of anything other than whether they were going to make it through the moment and live.

"COVER ME!" JAIME YELLED to Al then jumped up and ran in zigzags toward the back of the house while shots were fired his way. He got to the back door and yanked it open to dash through the kitchen, heading toward the room where he'd left Hank watching over Skippy.

The hallway was rubble. Most of the upper floor had crashed onto the first floor, which was a mound of splintered two-by-fours, broken sheets of drywall, and large chunks of flooring, plumbing, and what had once been roof.

He got to the door of the room where Skippy had been on his cot. He tried to enter and staggered back a step. Debris was piled up as high as six feet.

Jaime didn't hesitate. He rushed to the center of the pile and started digging, throwing bits of wood and plaster to either side, then some PVC pipes and flooring tiles.

He could hear shots still being exchanged outside, but he kept digging.

At last, he could see a leg then an arm. He kept lifting away broken, sharp-edged boards, chunks of plaster, and other debris, although his hands were sore and bleeding. When he had them uncovered enough, he felt for a pulse on both of them. Neither had one.

Hank had thrown himself across Skippy, apparently trying to protect him. They'd died together. Their deaths probably hadn't taken long.

Jaime went down on one knee, crossed himself—although he was as lapsed a Catholic as anyone could imagine—and said a short prayer that ended in a threat and a promise. "I will see that whoever did this dies as well. I swear this to you, my boys, my fierce fighting comrades."

He got to his feet, dizzy for a moment, and let rage and fury rush through him. Not bothering to brush the whitish dust and grime off himself, he spun and hurried to go back outside and join the others.

AL WAS GLAD THEY'D been able to keep Tanner from leaping up and charging right into the steady gunfire. He called out to the others, checking on their inventory of guns and ammo.

He didn't have to yell too loudly, since Barky and Maury, still holding Tanner down, had crawled closer until they were snugged up close to Al on one side. Bonnie, Maury, Phil, and Floy had crowded closer on the other side of Fergie.

Al looked up and saw Jaime come flying from around the back of the house. He'd seen Jaime like that before, like the *tick, tick, tick* of a bomb. He was ready to explode at any second. His face was red and flushed, and he was taking deep, gasping breaths as he ran. Not bothering to zig or zag, he had his gun out and was running toward the men shooting at them.

"Is your friend okay?" Barky asked Al.

"No, he's not okay. When he's like this, a whole lot of people are going to feel his wrath, if he doesn't get himself killed first. He'll be wanting to tear up this town."

"Get down, you fool!" Al yelled at Jaime.

But Jaime kept running. He had to pass close to their huddled group, so Al leaped up and tackled him.

Holding him was like trying to hold down a writhing, squirming maniac. He flipped Jaime over and saw a face contorted with anger.

"Let me go, Al. Let me at those sons o' bitches."

"You won't do anyone any good if you throw your life away. You've been in conflicts before and seen what happens when someone goes battle berserk," Al said. "Hank and Skippy?"

"Both dead."

That seemed to fire up Jaime again, and Al had his hands full, holding him down.

Floy crawled over to where they wrestled and slid on top, halfway smothering Al as well as Jaime.

"All right. All right." Jaime was coughing. "Let me breathe. I'll stop and think a bit. Use the leadership skills I'm supposed to possess."

Floy rolled off Al, and Al got off Jaime.

"Thanks," Al said to Jaime. "Thanks for calming down."

"Oh, I'm far from being calmed down. But you make sense. We need to help each other," Jaime said. "What's our ammo situation?"

"It sucks."

As if they'd just heard, two of the mercenaries jammed in fresh clips and rushed them, firing so often they were pinned to the ground.

Their own deaths would only be a matter of time, and not a very darned long time, unless they could do something.

Then Al heard honking.

He risked rising high enough to see a wave of pickup trucks pouring in through the front gate, their cabs and back ends filled with the locals Floy had called to help them.

Al wanted to cheer and wave a flag but knew they'd best stay hunkered down for a while more.

Chapter Twenty-Three

Cat couldn't believe it. Her men had been seconds away from eradicating the problem and wiping out the whole intrusive bunch of nosy busybodies when the horns of half a dozen pickup trucks started honking behind her. Men in the beds of the trucks were waving guns in the air, reminding her of those movie scenes where the villagers rose up and stormed the castle with torches and pitchforks.

Well, she damn well wasn't going to let that happen. She was standing behind the SUV as bullets bounced off the other side. Soon, bullets would be coming from the other direction too.

She climbed into the vehicle, slid into the driver's seat, and locked the doors. All she needed was her own mercenaries to run back and beat on the doors to be let in.

The engine started immediately, and she backed the SUV away from the sustained gunfire from two sides and turned right toward the approaching pickup trucks.

They'd formed a defensive line. She played chicken, aiming right at the one on the end. It veered off to one side, allowing her to power through the narrow gap.

Shots from both sides bounced off the windows and sides of the SUV, which after all was why she'd bought bulletproof ones.

She barreled through the gate and headed the only way she could, toward the town.

BONNIE STAYED HUNCHED down low, hugging the ground next to Al as shots continued to whiz over their heads from the two advancing mercenaries. She gave thanks that none of them had been hurt badly, although she'd heard Maury yip once. But he'd waved a hand at her, indicating that it wasn't bad. She saw Phil holding his forearm, too, but that was partly to aim his Western-style Colt and keep firing careful shots.

When the two advancing men in black were nearly upon them, Bonnie popped up and fired twice, taking out one of the men, who crumpled to the ground.

The other turned and ran the opposite way, just in time to see the SUV weaving through the line of pickup trucks. Those in the backs of the trucks jumped out, every one of them with a gun of some sort, and all of them ran toward the last of the mercenaries.

He fired into them in a long sweeping burst, and several fell to the ground. But the many he'd missed opened fire as they got closer, and the man in black jerked and twitched as bullets riddled him. He, too, fell to the earth.

The arriving pickup trucks pulled to a stop when they got close, and the drivers turned off the engines.

Bonnie still had her face pressed so close to the ground that she could smell the grass and the dirt beneath. She was sensing something, feeling it, but wasn't quite sure what it was. Then it registered. It was quiet, a silence where not even a bird dared chirp.

She turned her head and saw Tanner lift his muzzle and sniff the air. He was getting it, too, and neither Maury nor Barky bothered to push his head down again, out of the way of flying bullets. No more were zipping past their heads.

Then she did hear something, the sounds of feet on the ground as the arriving cavalry continued to run her way, and she could smell cordite in the air. But the conflict was over.

Phil and Floy were the first to stand and wave at the incoming horde.

"Give us a hand with the wounded!" Floy yelled. "I don't think anyone's hurt too bad. At least, I hope not."

Two of the drivers climbing out of the trucks had first aid kits and ran toward Floy, holding them in the air.

"Can someone give me a ride into town?" Jaime was shoving his cell phone into his pocket. "I have tactical squads already at work I'd like to join."

One of the truck drivers held up a hand, and Jaime started off with him.

But Jaime turned to Al as he passed. "Will you see to my two men, Al? I'll owe you big time."

"I think we're pretty square all around," Al said. "Of course I'll take care of Hank and Skippy. They were fine men."

Jaime started to say something but choked a bit and turned his head away. He picked up his pace as he and the volunteer went to a big black Ford pickup and climbed in. Soon, they were heading through the gate and out of sight.

With her years as a former nurse, Bonnie shoved her borrowed pistol under her belt and tended the wounded, whom Floy and other townspeople carried to her.

"Do me first," Phil said, "so Floy and I can lead our friends into town to do some much-needed cleaning up." He was pulling off his shirt, which was soaked through with blood on one side. He had a slender torso, more muscled than Bonnie had expected and with almost no chest hair, yet he still managed to look manly.

He caught Bonnie eyeing his chest. "I was a gym rat for years. I thought it would help me do better with the ladies. I was two-step dancing with this attractive gal once and was keeping my body stiff and flexed, so she could tell I worked out. I'd heard they like that. She told me, 'Hey, relax. Women don't want a hard body so much as they want a warm heart.' Wisest thing anyone ever told me."

He had a through-and-through shot that had just missed his clavicle. She washed out the wounds with bottled water Floy had brought her and cleaned them with some of the napkins he'd brought as well. Then she taped up both wounds.

The first aid kits she'd been given were store-bought, but they would do, since most weren't too seriously hurt. Bonnie had dealt with far worse. As soon as she was done patching up Phil, she started on Maury, who had a bullet crease along his upper left arm.

"You're lucky." Phil held up his bloodied shirt. "I'm going to need a wardrobe adjustment here."

"I've got a couple of spare shirts over in my Silverado," one of the wounded men waiting said. "I gotta warn you—one says Willie Nelson for President."

"I've worn worse." Phil jogged toward the truck.

The shirt donor looked up at Bonnie, holding a hand over a bullet crease in his forearm. "Do the others first," he told her. "Mine can wait. I've been hurt worse than this doing yard work." His teeth showed bright white in his thick black beard as he grinned.

As she tended to the other two wounded men, Bonnie noticed a pattern. They seemed jubilant about their recent victory but just a little embarrassed about not rising up and doing anything sooner.

"You know, Floy don't just cook the best grilled cheese sandwich to be found," one of them told her, "but he wound us up to get off our duffs." He was looking away, in part because he'd had to pull his pants and underwear down and also because he was one of those who couldn't look at his own blood as she cleaned and taped his wound.

"Shot in the buttock," he said. "I'm not even gonna tell anyone I was hit unless they want to kiss the wound."

The other man had been shot in the hand and was going to need some professional attention. Bonnie got him patched up enough to be taken to the ER, which was probably going to be a busy place.

She looked toward the gate. None of the men in pickups had tried to chase that Cat woman. But she was heading straight into town, which was probably a hornets' nest, from what Bonnie had heard from the other fresh arrivals.

But only two of the mercenaries' bodies were there. She wondered what had become of the third.

Chapter Twenty-Four

Cat drove the SUV as far as she dared into the edge of town, painfully aware that even though it was bulletproof, it had a lot of marks on it from being in a real shoot-out. An APB was almost certainly out for black SUVs.

As soon as she saw the flashing lights of all manner of law enforcement activity going on ahead, she snapped a turn onto the next side street and got ready to ditch the vehicle.

She reached for her Louis Vuitton suitcase and briefcase. Only the suitcase was still there.

"Why, that low-down, thieving—" She could have gone on for quite a while, cussing Max and wishing him dead in all manner of the nastiest ways possible, but she saw a couple of members of some sort of SWAT team carrying guns and looking down each street.

She clambered out of the SUV, locked it, and started off down the street, staying as close to any tree or structure as she could.

When she got within a block or two of the chop shop, she hesitated. The place was swarming with combat-gear cops as thick as ants.

She practically tiptoed up to the row of cars that had been waiting to go inside and become spare parts. Then she realized that acting stealthy could work against her, so she stood upright and walked with a more casual ease toward her goal, just a dumpy little lady on a stroll with a suitcase. Once there, she gave the cars a quick look. The last one in the row would do, an almost new green Kia Soul, not the sort of car she would normally want, but that made it perfect. It was unlocked, and the keys were inside.

"Slow and easy," she kept telling herself as she neared the edge of town.

Roadblocks might be up already and not ones formed by the cops she'd owned.

In the previous two towns, she'd used up the opportunities for grabbing cash until the area was milked dry. She hadn't experienced anything like the resistance she'd just seen. She had smoothly moved in then as easily segued out. This time had been far from smooth. Maybe she was losing her grip or her precise awareness of her situation. She caught herself picking up speed and made herself slow down.

Being patient was hard, though, because she was boiling inside.

She was mad—furious—and had a new purpose: vengeance. *Those people did this to me. Those blasted people.*

THE GUNFIGHT HAD STILL been at its peppiest when Max slipped inside the SUV to look at his eye in the rearview mirror. He'd feared he might lose the eye, but it was only swollen tightly shut, so he was ready to go out and fight beside his men. Then those trucks had arrived. They changed everything, and he made a snap decision. Max grabbed the briefcase and slipped out of the SUV on the side opposite Cat.

He kept low in a flat crawl across the open stretch of lawn and into the early rough along the woods on the grounds. Once he could rise, in the cover of denser growth, he could move faster. He knew where every trip wire, laser beam, and occasional camera was placed. He'd put them there.

He unlocked the side gate and locked it again behind himself to slow anyone who tried to follow. As soon as he could, he crossed the road into the green belt there, where he hugged the trees as he passed through the woods, slowly working his way back to town. Trucks went by, some headed back to Port Dexter. At each sound of an engine, he hugged the other side of a tree and glanced down at the briefcase.

Max had seen combat action in Africa, Asia, and the Middle East. He doubted the coastal woodlands of Texas could throw anything worse at him. Still, if he was spotted, that could all change.

When he heard a vehicle's tires chewing at the asphalt of the road, he ducked or dived the way he had when avoiding incoming fire. He let his training and instincts take over. All he had to do was get to town and find a way out, and he had all the time in the world to do that right and not get caught.

He'd expected much more when he was hired by that woman. At the very least, he'd hoped for sex. Max certainly had not expected to be sleeping on a cot with the others like some boot camp grunt.

In every one of the three continents where he'd seen combat action, he'd been treated better and rewarded more richly than he had by her. Only in the final days of his Port Dexter experience did he realize what a one-way street her sense of loyalty was: do as she said and expect nothing in return.

Looking around, he still had a long way to go. He needed to find someplace to hide and wait if he was to escape that cursed town. As the sky got darker, his black outfit would help. At the moment, it was not an asset and was bloody uncomfortable as the day grew even hotter.

But he bent and patted the briefcase. With his stealth and survival skills, he would get through this, and for the first time, doing so was worth it.

AS THEY HEADED TOWARD the pickup trucks that had come to their rescue, Al thought the clouds seemed to be breaking up as though after a storm, although it hadn't rained. They separated to frame a growing expanse of robin-egg sky.

Maury and Bonnie climbed into a truck owned by Floy's barber, Mikey, who talked the whole time about how much he loved Floy's chicken-fried steaks.

"I eat three to five a week," he said, and his build backed his statement.

Barky and Luke Boy got into that truck as well, since Mikey had promised to drop them off at their shrimp boat.

Al, Fergie, and Tanner slid into the extended cab of a big GMC pickup owned by one of Floy's pals, Ernesto, who couldn't stop grinning. Floy sat in the front seat. They'd had to leave his food truck behind for the time being, since it still wore something of a bull's-eye for any of the wrong sort left.

Their truck slid into the small convoy of pickups heading back to town. Fergie put her hand in Al's and squeezed. Tanner tried to push between them, but Fergie didn't loosen her grip.

Floy turned in his seat to look back at Al and Fergie. "You shouldn't hold it against the people of Port Dexter that they didn't rise up sooner. There were disappearances involving anyone who started to protest."

"My *tio* was one," Ernesto said. "He complained. Poof, he was gone."

"These were very bad people," Floy said. "We all knew that from the start. They put their own police people in right away. When they took over the sheriff's department, too, we knew we'd better lie low until we had a legitimate chance to change things. You guys showing up flipped the switch that needed switching."

"All we wanted to do was find out what was going on and report it," Fergie said.

"You did way more than that."

"What're you going to do now?" Al asked.

"We wanted to attack the police station. Weed out all the fake cops," Floy said.

"You know they are probably all ex-cons, don't you?" Al asked.

"We figured something like that. Most of them were as mean as two-headed snakes." Floy chuckled. "But man alive, they sure did like to eat. I saw a lot of them."

"Anyways," Ernesto said, "the police building is already surrounded by some of the real law enforcement, mostly federal folks so far. So we're hoping to chase down and catch any of the fake police left."

"It'll be a real switch for us to be the ones chasing cop cars. We may not be able to corner any of them until they run out of gas, but none of us fancy having to talk to the media who will soon be swarming the area. After all, we aren't official and probably shouldn't even be running around with guns like wild-eyed vigilantes." Floy grinned. "But we kinda just want to feel and savor the sense of freedom in our own town. Then we'll all go home and hopefully pretend none of this happened."

"I hear you," Fergie said. "All we want is to go home too."

Chapter Twenty-Five

Jaime Avila sat stewing in the passenger seat. The driver, Chet, another of Floy's faithful patrons, said he worked at the local shrimp-processing plant and smelled like he'd just come from work. He stopped his truck where several other pickups of the rescuing cavalry had pulled up near the police station. The driver looked disappointed to see ICE vans pulled up in front of the yellow brick building, which was both dirty and far from new.

"Ah, man. You guys kinda swooped in and scooped us here. We was hoping to get a little payback on these guys who made our lives hell for a stretch."

"I do understand," Jaime said. "Believe me. The feeling is alive inside me right now."

"Well, if you get a chance, put in a lick for me, okay?"

"Will do."

"I mean it."

"Me too. Thanks for the ride." Jaime got out and walked past the other pickups.

The locals behind the wheels were staring at the police station and probably playing newsreels in their heads of what they would have done to those inside.

Elliot, Jaime's second-in-command, was waiting for him just outside the front door. He was in full tactical-force gear, though he apparently hadn't even needed to draw his gun.

Jaime was overly aware of the shape his own clothes were in. The crisply ironed black shirt he'd worn was rumpled and covered in a layer of grime from digging at the house.

"I was sorry as hell to hear about Hank and Skippy," Elliot said as they shook hands. "I've sent a detail out that way to bring them back. Okay?"

Jaime nodded and followed Elliot inside.

"We've got them all. Do you want to see a sample?" Elliot waved a hand toward an interrogation room.

Inside, a small guy still in his police uniform sat on one side of a metal table, while one of Jaime's men sat on the other side.

Jaime took in the name tag on the cop, which read Adams. "I suppose that's not his real name."

"No, it isn't," Elliot said. "He comes back as one Fletcher Briskon, an ex-con who just happens to have two outstanding bench warrants, not to mention he's in parole violation for wearing a gun." To the cop, he said, "This is Jaime Avila, our ticked-off boss."

The fake cop looked up at Jaime with an Elvis sneer on his face. "Isn't Jaime a girl's name?"

Jaime's fist flew forward in a flash and hit the fake cop on the nose, which began to bleed at once. Then he handed the guy his white handkerchief.

"Wad you do that for?" the fake cop asked past the handkerchief he pressed to his nose.

"Because there aren't any more of those bastards in black around to punch," Jaime said. "And you've got a smart mouth that's going to get a chance to turn back into a prison whisper."

Jaime stared at the prisoner, who flinched, probably thinking Jaime was loading up to pop him one again.

Elliot led him out of the room and closed the door. "Didn't you let us know you think one of them slipped away?"

Jaime felt his frown wrestling against a flicker of a smile trying to get past his barely suppressed smoldering anger. "Hope springs eternal," he said, "unless someone beats me to him."

Chapter Twenty-Six

"**A**re you okay with us going out shrimping, just the two of us?" Barky asked, standing on the deck of his shrimp boat with Luke Boy.

The other man shrugged and kept coiling a rope. "We've done it before."

"Then let's go."

"Okay, sir."

The gulls were making a clatter of noise and rising to flutter around the boat. They were ready for it to go out into the briny gulf and do some real shrimping once more.

The clouds at dusk had something of an attitude, pushing the blue to one side, maybe hinting of a storm, and the sea felt kind of rough, but Barky sure felt good to be bouncing across the waves once they were going.

He set a course for his favorite place, not too far out yet with enough promise to haul in a large load of shrimp.

Luke Boy hustled around, getting all the gear ready to drop the trawler's nets. Barky would have to tie the wheel and rush down to give him a hand now and again, but they could get through it.

He felt a thrill of pleasure at just being able to do the job he knew well, to have the usual anxiety of whether they would fill their nets or not. None of that was easy, but that was okay.

Barky was relieved to be done with the masquerade of hauling some crates out to the gulf and others back in, not knowing or wanting to know what was in them. He hadn't been one of those picking up loads of young women, girls really, who'd been rounded up by coyotes and promised a wonderful life in America, only to find themselves in a state of slavery and prostitution. But the worst had been those trips carrying handcuffed men out to the deeps of the gulf, only to come back without them. Those men in the black combat outfits had been along each time for that, and he'd feared for his life and Luke Boy's each time.

He checked his bearings and righted his course, looking ahead at the waves and swells, which were higher and rougher than usual. The wind was raspy rough and looked like it wanted to get even more playful. It probably would before darkness set all the way in. He'd been through worse, but the effort was going to take his full attention.

When he glanced down at the deck, he blinked, thinking he was seeing things. He imagined he'd seen one of those men in black. He looked again. One of them was surely standing there, and he had one arm around Luke Boy. In that hand was a briefcase, and in the other was a gun pointed at his first mate's head. One of the guy's eyes was swollen shut into a puffy, narrow red-and-black slit. Luke Boy had done that with his slingshot.

"I want you to forget fishing and take us up the coast to drop me off. You understand?"

Barky realized that the man in black was that Max Varon fellow the others had told him about, the leader of those cutthroats, a pirate in modern times, and nobody to take lightly. He wasn't a man who'd killed just one or two but perhaps hundreds of others.

Luke Boy, his eyes open wide, was scared down to the toes of his rubber boots.

"I hear you!" Barky yelled. "I'll have to turn her a bit."

As he turned the wheel slowly, watching how the bow hit the waves, he reached and worked the lever that brought up the outriggers.

"What are you doing?" Max yelled as the boat pitched from side to side as its outriggers lifted.

"Just turning her."

Even Luke Boy, an experienced hand wearing rubber boots, was having a hard time standing upright as the wind grabbed the raised nets on either side and rocked the boat harder and harder. For the first time, Barky was glad the sea was cutting up so rough.

At one hard, slamming jerk, the boat tilted dangerously to one side. Max's hands flew away from Luke Boy, and he dropped the briefcase.

With the boat still pitching and yawing, he bent to grab for the briefcase and stumbled like a drunken sailor.

Luke Boy waited until he was behind the mercenary, put his hands on Max's back, and pushed hard, sending him all the way to the gunwale and over it with a jerk.

Max's gun hand waved all around, but he hadn't had a chance to fire.

Luke Boy rushed for one of the lifesaver rings.

"Don't you dare!" Barky yelled. He started the downriggers back into place, and the boat steadied as they gripped the water like claws. He kept the boat moving along in the direction they'd been going. "Bring that briefcase up here."

Luke Boy came to the helm, carrying the Louis Vuitton briefcase. "Should we go back for him? I don't know how to feel about that, pushing a guy into the gulf. It was bad enough when it was them doing it." He looked a little green at the gills.

Barky had already started the laborious process of slowing to turn the boat around. "You've got a good heart in you, boy. I guess I don't care much for the idea of us turning into ruthless men like them either."

When they got to the spot where the man had gone overboard, he could spot nothing except wave on wave climbing each other as they had done for most of his life.

"A big guy like that shouldn't wear so much gear if he's gonna go for a swim," Barky said.

"Yep." Luke Boy's eyes were sad, though.

"You'll get over it and maybe even feel good about it in time."

Barky could have summoned several stories from his navy days when it was him or someone else. But this wasn't about him—it was about Luke Boy.

"This was one very bad man," Barky said. "I'll bet that guy was biting sharks on the way down. Don't feel bad. You deserve a pat on the back and maybe a handsome reward."

His first mate was looking away, not having anything further to say. Several good days on the water and getting some good hauls of shrimp should fix that in time.

Barky looked at the briefcase Luke Boy was holding, which looked very nice. "Open it up."

Luke Boy did, and his eyes popped open wide as he gasped. It was full of money—bundles and bundles of hundred-dollar bills.

Barky grinned, and so did his mate when he looked up.

"You know, Luke Boy, I do believe we might just get ourselves one o' them big hundred-foot freezer shrimp boats and stay out for a month at a time like the big boys do."

Chapter Twenty-Seven

"I'm going to call again," Bonnie said.

Fergie glanced back at her. She understood. Bonnie was fidgety and eager.

"We'll be there in ten minutes," Fergie said. "Why don't you hold your horses and focus on how happy Little Al is going to be to see you."

Bonnie frowned then smiled. "Okay. Okay. After all we been through, I guess I can wait a few ticks for the icing on the cake." She slid over in the back seat and gave Maury a hug.

"It's nice being just us again." Al rubbed behind Tanner's ears. "Seems like we've had a constant crowd around for quite a spell."

"I'm glad we paused to have a warm lunch before we hit the road. That Floy can plain cook, can't he?" Maury said.

He'd provided four box lunches for them: fried chicken, deep-fried deviled eggs, and fried pickles as well as hush puppies. Tanner had been awarded his own box of sautéed chicken tenderloins. He'd beaten them all at eating his share as they rolled along the highway between Port Dexter and Port Aransas.

Al spelled Fergie long enough for her to eat while he drove, but she got back behind the steering wheel of her car as soon as she could.

She felt good driving her own car somewhere other than into danger. They were going home. As much as she tried not to, though, she found herself thinking about that Catahoula Cathy Castleton. That crazy ol' gal was out in the world somewhere, free, even after all the horrific things she'd done were slowly coming to light as a piranha-hungry media got the details. The story of her smuggling underage girls into America for her brothels trickled out from federal agencies, which were still turning over every stone in Port Dexter and frantically looking for her everywhere.

She must've made a fortune stealing the cash and cars from hundreds of men who were never seen again, many of whom had been dropped alive into a cold sea and left there to die. Millions in cash had been in the two SUVs stopped on the highway by a couple of the FBI's Critical Incident Response teams heading from Houston to Port Dexter. Special Agent Danielle Cassidy was leading them, since human trafficking was involved. Nobody knew what kind of resources that Cat woman had amassed over the years. She probably had offshore and overseas accounts full of money harvested in similar ways at other cities. The feds were still unraveling the woman's dark past.

Jaime's presence had turned out to be advantageous, too, since she had been laundering cash for the cartels. But he still wasn't over losing two of his closest men. He and the other feds were scouring the country, looking for that Cat woman.

For some reason, above the murmur and the whir of asphalt beneath her tires, Fergie heard a song playing in her head. It was Amy Winehouse singing "I'm No Good."

Fergie had a pretty good hunch why that particular earworm had chosen that moment to intrude on her simple joy at heading back toward their house.

"When I get home," Fergie said, "I'm going to lie down and sleep for about a week."

"With no fooling around?" Maury asked.

She winked at Al. "Hardly any."

As soon as their tires crunched on gravel as they pulled into Mary Doughrety's motel,

Bonnie opened her door, eager to rush inside and scoop up Little Al.

Fergie saw that, in lieu of her usual Chief's Special shoved under her belt, Bonnie had the standard police Smith & Wesson she'd gotten from one of the fake cops there.

"Are you going to wear that constantly?" Fergie asked.

"Until we get safely home and are snug in our house, yep." Bonnie grinned.

But she waited while the others got out of the car and Al clipped a leash onto Tanner.

Bonnie led the way into the motel office and didn't pause to knock at the open doorway leading to Mary's living quarters. She was the first through, with the others as close behind as could be.

When Bonnie came to an abrupt halt, Fergie was so close that she bumped into Bonnie's back, and Al bumped into Fergie. Fergie was tall enough to see past Bonnie.

Catahoula Cathy was standing beside a straight-backed wooden chair, to which Mary Doughrety was duct taped, with a piece of the silver tape across her mouth. Her eyes were pleading, and her face had flushed pink. Her dyed-blond hair was tousled and stood out in several directions. Patty Belle was taped in the same manner on a similar chair beside Mary. Her mouth wasn't taped shut, though, since she couldn't speak. But she couldn't use her bound hands to sign to Bonnie. Her eyes bulged as she tried to nod with them toward the woman who'd bound them.

Cat held Little Al up with one arm around his papoose, the barrel of a pistol pressed right against the side of his head.

He squealed and reached out with both chubby arms toward Bonnie. Tanner growled low in his throat and tugged at his leash.

"Now, don't anybody do anything stupid, you hear?" Cat said.

Fergie glanced around. None of them had a sidearm except for the Smith & Wesson shoved under Bonnie's belt. But she wouldn't get to it in time.

Bonnie's face was as flushed as Mary's, whom she pointed at with her left hand. "I made a mistake with that one. I tried to replace a fear with a greater fear. I was wrong. Fear is fear, no matter how you slice it."

"She didn't rat you out," Cat said. "Thanks, in part, to your little deaf-and-dumb special-needs friend here."

She waved toward Patty Belle and might've tightened her grip on Little Al. His eyes popped, and he squealed louder. Tanner bounced on the end of his leash, growling and pulling.

Fergie halfway expected Bonnie to charge across the room at that, regardless of her chances. But Bonnie seemed cooler than Fergie had expected. She noticed that in the exchange of words, Bonnie's hand had moved up to almost touch the butt of the gun at her waist.

"So your fear did outweigh mine for a bit, but in the end, I'm smarter," Cat said. "When I didn't hear from her, and you didn't have your little brat with you, I knew—"

"Why you—" Maury, fists clenched, took a step, ready to rush forward.

"Stand down, Maury," Al said. "This isn't the time."

Bonnie's hand was closer to the butt of her pistol. She needed another half second. A Smith & Wesson like the one at her waist was a double-action gun. Bonnie wouldn't even have to pull the hammer back, just get it up in time.

Fergie said, "If I were you, Cat woman, I'd have just slipped away into the night and enjoyed all the ill-gotten money you've surely stowed away by now. But looking at how you live, I know you aren't capable of that. It's all about grabbing and getting with you, saving every little bit like some squirrel with its nuts."

"Are you calling me names?"

"If I were, it would be to call you a greedy, revenge-driven puddle of pus."

Cat blinked, and her mouth started to open.

Suddenly, Patty Belle let out her enormous goose sound in a loud "Honk!"

Cat's eyes shifted to her and opened wider.

At the same second, Al let go of Tanner's leash.

Cat swung her gun away from Little Al to Fergie then toward the rushing dog before realizing the real threat was Bonnie, who was raising her gun. Cat swung the barrel back to the baby at the same second Bonnie fired.

A dot appeared in Cat's forehead, a trickle of red, and she was falling.

As Little Al dropped toward the floor from her limp hand, Maury was across the room, diving to catch his son before he hit the floor.

AL RUSHED TO GRAB TANNER'S leash to pull him away before he could maul what was already a corpse before Cat's body hit the floor.

Maury held the baby close to his chest and tried to soothe away his crying. Bonnie put the Smith & Wesson down on the floor and squatted to hug both Maury and Little Al.

Fergie had to step around Catahoula Cathy's body to get to Mary. She pulled off the silver strip across Mary's mouth first so that she could speak. Then she moved to free Patty Belle. As soon as she was free, she shot across the room to crowd into the huddle and tried to get her pudgy little arms around Bonnie, Maury, and the baby all at the same time.

Even while Fergie moved back to free Mary's wrists and ankles, the motel owner nodded down toward Bonnie. "Anything that woman *ever* tells me, I'm gonna believe. She has more backbone, grit, and willingness to do what needs doing more than the rest of Texas."

Al had stepped into the motel's office to use the phone. "Jaime, I have some news for you. We've located Catahoula Cathy."

"Just tell me where, and I'll copter there in a flash. Where, Al? Where?"

"Well, first I've got to tell you something. You see, Bonnie—"

"Oh my heavenly stars. You let that crack shot near someone I was hoping to deal with personally."

"There wasn't much time for a choice. And, well, you know Bonnie."

Jaime sighed. "I believe, in that case, I'll pass the info on to Danielle Cassidy. The FBI has the biggest case to make against her, and ol' Danny could use the feather in her cap. The DEA is already trying to horn in over a few kilos of seriously pure coke that showed up in those vans the FBI stopped."

"By 'few,' you mean—"

"Enough for the DEA to get all nosy and bothered, Al. Looks like those shrimp boats weren't just bringing in underage girls. It was pretty good cover for one very big money operation, one that's all over now."

Al went back into Mary's living quarters, where Tanner was crowded in close to Bonnie, Maury, and Patty Belle, all with wet, shiny cheeks and clutching Little Al, who'd quit crying and was smiling and reaching for Maury's nose. Maury was keeping a tight grip on Tanner's leash to keep him away from the body, which was acting as a centerpiece to the room.

Mary, Fergie, and Al stood side by side, looking down at the body. Mary rubbed at sticky silver flecks on her wrists from the tape.

Al was thinking about the immense wealth the woman on the floor had possessed at one point, though she'd made herself live in something near abject poverty while wanting more, more, more.

"You know"—Bonnie gave the baby, Patty Belle, and Maury another squeeze—"there are times and events in life that seem designed to let you really realize what's most important in your life."

Mary looked awkward and unsure. A good while would pass before whatever federal bunch was coming would arrive and make the rest of her day an ordeal. She went over to the kitchen that ran along one wall to make tea.

Fergie stepped closer to Al and put an arm around his waist.

Al knew about the members of his household, but he wondered if Jaime would be as obsessed about finding Max and avenging his two fallen men as had Catahoula Cathy, who had bothered to come after them when she could've been on the far side of the planet instead. He thought of poor old Bobby Ray Champion, who'd wanted fame and a bounce back to his career but had been doomed to the slippery slope of his habits.

He didn't feel preachy about a damned thing, though, just tired, hungry, and ready to roll the rest of the way home. But come to that, he looked at his family, dog and all, and he felt happy. He would focus on that until he could get home again, like Odysseus after his thrashing around for all those years before he could make it back to where he lived.

Chapter Twenty-Eight

After a solid week of looking, of turning over every rock he could and following every hint of a lead, Jamie Avila had not uncovered the slightest bit of anything that could lead him to Max Varon.

He went into his office wearing a black suit, a white shirt, and a black tie, having just come from Skippy's funeral. He hadn't expected that attending would make him feel any better, and it hadn't. He'd been relentless, obsessed with finding the man who'd killed Hank and Skippy.

A few of his colleagues had hinted he'd gone a bit Captain Ahab about it, but they stopped when they saw the look on his face.

He opened the closet and started taking off his suit to switch into his work uniform.

Something on his desk caught his eye, a flash of yellow and orange—the edge of a bright postcard sticking out of his pile of mail.

He paused and reached for it. The picture was of a shrimp trawler at sunset, the sky bright orange and yellow. Birds flew in swarms close around the vessel.

Jaime flipped it over. That was his address, all right. But the message made him stop and think.

In scratchings close to a crayon's work, someone had written *Max* in block letters followed by an equals sign that pointed to a crude drawing of a fish, the sort seen on the backs of cars. The brief cryptic message was signed with an anchor.

He shook his head then, in a burst, fully understood. Max was sleeping with the fishes.

Anger swept through him first, a flash of raging fire, and he tossed the card onto his desk and clenched his fists. Someone had done what he'd wanted to do himself, had beaten him to it. But just as suddenly, a calm swept through him. He picked up the card again and smiled.

He knew who, but he was darned if he knew why or, especially, how. But sending the card had been a kindness. Jaime could ease up, knowing that somehow, however crazy and impossible, one old navy sailor had done an honor to another navy veteran and had avenged Skippy. He let out a long, slow breath, and with it, every ounce of tension seemed to go out of him.

AL LIFTED HIS MUG AND took a sip of coffee. It had gone cold, but that was okay. The day was a warm one.

He sat on the upper porch of his lakeside house, which looked out across Lake Travis. The horizon was shifting its way through bars of orange and purple as the sun was slowly disappearing.

Fergie sat in the chair nearest his, with Tanner at their feet. Bonnie sat on the other side of Fergie, holding Little Al sleeping on her lap. Patty Belle was pressed as close as she could get to Bonnie's side, with her head resting on one shoulder.

"You know you're going to have to let go of him now and again, or he's going to grow up smothered with affection," Fergie said.

"That's okay. Patty Belle will be heading off to that deaf school soon enough for her short stint and will come back all eager to help tend to the little rascal, and I'll let her. It'll just be for a while until I ease up on the appreciation of getting to hold him at all myself and see him grow up."

Fergie smiled and shook her head.

Al finished the last of his coffee and put his mug on the wooden floor beside his chair.

The sun was almost gone. The horizon had become a thin orange line and soon would be dark. He could make out the beginning of stars and a sliver of a moon.

"Hey, you guys!" Maury yelled from inside the house. "Listen to this." He turned up the radio.

Al could make out scraps of Bobby Ray Champion's voice. A demo cassette tape of him singing an early version of the Port Dexter song he'd been struggling to write had been found in that sad heap of a car of his. The Austin recording studio that had handled Bobby Ray's past CDs had remastered it and worked their magic on it, and it was a hit because of Port Dexter still being in the news weeks after one of the biggest cleanups of a town in recent Texas history.

"Well, Bobby Ray got what he wanted in the end: fame," Al said.

"And the proceeds are going to a substance abuse charity, so it's a win-win," Fergie said. "Good for him."

"I saw Phil Rosenbeirn's picture in the news," Bonnie said. "Hilarious. Him, elected sheriff in that special election."

"And Floy's the new mayor," Fergie said. "Don't forget that. Equally comic, but couldn't be more deserving. I loved his platform: clear our beaches and restore family tourism. That's a win-win for all down there."

"Those guys sure stepped up and are part of the reason we're here to talk about it," Al said. "I'm surprised they didn't ask me to be sheriff."

"They asked one of us." Fergie turned to grin at him.

"You?"

"No. Her." She pointed at Bonnie.

"Really?"

"Aw, they were just givin' me a hat tip, said I was a shootist, the kind of sheriff they were lookin' for. Truth is, they were just sayin' a thanks for being shed of that Cat woman."

"You did do the job there," Fergie said.

"I'm sure the way they probably have what happened pictured was a combination of the OK Corral and Gary Cooper in *High Noon*. Who I did it for was this little fellow here, who I'm about to take inside for Maury, since it's his turn. Did you ever think there'd be a day, Al, when your horndog of a brother would be changing diapers?"

"Can't say that I ever did." Al shook his head. "And now I can't get the picture out of my head."

Tanner got up and moved closer to plop down against Al's leg, as warm as it was. Patty Belle still stayed as close to Bonnie as she could. Al had seen her looking around at the house when they came home. She seemed full of wonder and appreciation at having lived to see it again. They'd all felt a little of that.

Their morning had been one of those memorable moments to savor, bursting upon them like a ripe fruit. The sky glittered with the remaining glow of stars and a sliver of a moon, evolving into a rich, cloudless blue sky. A light breeze from across the lake blew cool against the growing heat of the day. The coffee, made from freshly ground Guatemalan beans, had a deep, hearty flavor with no hint of bitterness. So the day had gone, with good food, naps, and not a single person chasing them or shooting at them all day. Now, night seemed ready to tuck them in like a dark blanket.

"Well, I don't know about you guys," Fergie said, "but I'll be okay if we don't go anywhere for a while, unless it's fishing on the lake. I just want to stay home a spell and listen to the crickets."

"Amen," Al and Bonnie said at the same time.

About the Author

Russ Hall is author of fifteen published fiction books, most in hardback and subsequently published in mass market paperback by Harlequin's Worldwide Mystery imprint and Leisure Books. He has also co-authored numerous non-fiction books, most recently *Do You Matter: How Great Design Will Make People Love Your Company* (Financial Times Press, 2009) with Richard Brunner, former head of design at Apple, *Now You're Thinking* (Financial Times Press, 2011), and *Identity* (Financial Times Press, 2012) with Stedman Graham, Oprah's companion.

His graduate degree is in creative writing. He has been a nonfiction editor for major publishing companies, ranging from HarperCollins (then Harper & Row), Simon & Schuster, to Pearson. He has lived in Columbus, OH, New Haven, CT, Boca Raton, FL, Chapel Hill, NC, and New York City. Moving to the Austin area from New York City in 1983.

He is a long-time member of the Mystery Writers of America, Western Writers of America, and Sisters in Crime. He is a frequent judge for writing organizations.

In 2011, he was awarded the Sage Award, by The Barbara Burnett Smith Mentoring Authors Foundation—a Texas award for the mentoring author who demonstrates an outstanding spirit of service in mentoring, sharing and leading others in the mystery writing community. In 1996, he won the Nancy Pickard Mystery Fiction Award for short fiction.

Read more at www.russhall.com.

About the Publisher

Dear Reader,

We hope you enjoyed this book. Please consider leaving a review on your favorite book site.

Visit https://RedAdeptPublishing.com to see our entire catalogue.

Check out our app for short stories, articles, and interviews. You'll also be notified of future releases and special sales.

www.ingramcontent.com/pod-product-compliance
Lightning Source LLC
Chambersburg PA
CBHW030625190726
48286CB00008B/2401